21

HENRIETTA'S WAR

by the same author

AND THEN THERE WAS ONE

HENRIETTA'S WAR

NEWS FROM THE HOME FRONT
1939–1942

JOYCE DENNYS

ANDRE DEUTSCH

The author and publisher
gratefully acknowledge permission granted
by the *Illustrated London News*
Archive and Picture Library to reproduce
material which originally appeared
in the *Sketch*.

This collection first published by
André Deutsch Limited
105 Great Russell Street London WC1

British Library Cataloguing in Publication Data
Dennys, Joyce
  Henrietta's war: news from the home front.
  1939–1942.
  I. Title
  828'.91408   PR6054.E49/
  ISBN 0-233-97829-1

Printed in Great Britain by
Ebenezer Baylis & Son Limited
The Trinity Press, Worcester, and London

To Pippa

In 1939 Joyce Dennys was living in Budleigh Salterton with her GP husband, their daughter and the family dog. As a young woman (she was already in her forties when the Second World War broke out) Miss Dennys had been to art school and she had published drawings in a glossy magazine, now defunct, called the *Sketch*. It was to the *Sketch* that she sent her first article. It was in the form of a letter to an imaginary friend fighting at the front and its purpose was as much to make city-dwellers realise what their country cousins were up to as to cheer the troops with news from home. After all, the citizens of Budleigh Salterton were also part of the historic drama. They too had loved ones at risk. They too were fired with patriotic feeling.

The article was such a success that Joyce Dennys was asked for more, and her letters to Robert became a regular feature of the magazine till the end of the war. In this little volume we have made a selection from the first two years, ending with Christmas 1941. The reader may like to know that though most of the letters are reproduced in their original form, some have been shortened and a few have been run together so that choice passages could be saved without appearing as fragments.

It should also be revealed that in this correspondence, in which Miss Dennys recreated herself in the character of Henrietta, all the characters except her husband Charles, her daughter Linnet and Perry the dog are invented. Real as they may seem (and every stout lady within miles of Budleigh Salterton thought herself the model for Lady B), they are creatures of fiction.

It is astonishing that with such powers of invention Joyce Dennys did not become a novelist. As it was she continued to paint and there were, apparently, one or two distantly remembered stage plays during the twenties. There was also a very charming little memoir *And Then There Was One* published only last year by Tabb House of Padstow in Cornwall.

Now over ninety, and still living in Budleigh Salterton, this enchantingly youthful old lady speaks wistfully of the encouragement girls and young women get nowadays to 'do their own thing'. One suspects she was too much cherished and relied on as wife, mother and friend to do quite everything she wanted. Yet how many liberated young women of today will leave a legacy of such overwhelming charm and unique historical interest as *Henrietta's War*?

I never do Spring Cleaning. I know I should and every year am filled with a longing to do better and rush round the house emptying drawers and shelves onto the floor and unearthing many treasures such as my dark glasses (mourned as lost) and endless snapshots. After enjoying several holidays in retrospect I somehow lose heart and bundle everything back again.

But this year I was rewarded for my good intentions by discovering a bundle of pieces I had written during the War for the *Sketch* magazine. The cuttings were anything but tidy, the margins thick with arrows, stars and balloons. But they were still readable and it was enthralling to be reminded of the privations and discomforts suffered by those living in what Authority was pleased to call a Safe Area. It made fascinating reading.

'Did we really do those peculiar things?' I said to my friend Caroline who had dropped in and was reading over my shoulder.

'We certainly did,' she said.

'Did we really parade the streets at night wearing tin hats?'

'Of course we did,' said Caroline. 'Look here, Joyce, I've got a daughter who is in publishing. Why don't you send these things to her – she won't mind the balloons.'

And that's exactly what I did.

Devon, 1985

October 18, 1939

M Y DEAR ROBERT
It was good to get your letter and hear that you are in a 'perfectly safe place', though I wonder how much of that is true and how much intended to allay the alarms of your Childhood's Friend. And why, when I and everybody else know that you are in France, must I address my letters to Berkshire? Well, well, I suppose They Know Best, and Ours Not to Reason Why, but I seem to remember that when I wrote to you in the last war I used to put 'B.E.F.,* France', quite boldly on the envelope, thereby no doubt endangering the safety of the British Empire.

I think there is a tendency in our generation to adopt a superior, know-all attitude towards this war just because we happen to have been through the last one, which the young must find maddening. Charles and I fight against it, not always successfully, I'm afraid. Lady B was here yesterday. Her view of the 'Ah, my dears, this is all very different from the last Dear Ol I War' brigade is bracing, to say the least. I saw Bill and Linnet exchange a satisfied look as she leaned further and further forward

Leaned further and further forward

in her excitement. Bill is waiting for a commission, and Linnet is going into hospital as a probationer. I won't write any more about them now or this letter will fail as a message of cheer for a middle-aged colonel on the Western Front. Next week I shall be able to write about them more calmly. One gets used to anything in time.

*British Expeditionary Force

Here we go on much as usual and one feels faintly ashamed of being in such a safe area. Charles says, 'How do you know it *is* a safe area?' and, of course, we don't. We don't know much about anything—yet. But in the meantime we have been told it is a safe area, and one is thankful not to have to start being frightened before one need. Freddie writes that in London everybody's ears are growing *straight* out of the sides of their heads with listening.

I feel this letter will not be complete without a word about our refugees. The day they were due to arrive, Charles and I had to go to a funeral at the other end of the county, which, incidentally, did nothing to raise our drooping spirits, but we left the Linnet in charge, with instructions that when the little fellow arrived she was to examine his head (Charles's suggestion this, doctors are inclined to look on the sordid side of life, aren't they?), give him a nice hot bath, an egg for his supper, tuck him up in bed, and write a heartening letter to his mother. The Linnet, who has not been head girl at school for nothing, took these duties seriously, even going so far as to lay a bar of chocolate on the lonely pillow and fish her old teddy-bear out of a box in the attic. At half-past five a youth of sixteen, just under six feet tall, was deposited on our doorstep. Linnet said she just managed to get the teddy-bear out in time. He ate the chocolate. His name is Bertram, and we have the whole Technical School billeted in the village. All such nice boys, but you can't feed them on ten shillings a week—at least, I suppose you *could*, but it wouldn't be quite kind. How eminently sensible is Mrs Whinebite, who has taken in all her rich relations as Pee-ing G's—thus, in the words of J. M. Barrie, 'turning her necessity to glorious gain'.

My dear Robert, I have a great urge to knit something for you! I suppose you are overrun, or, rather overwrapped with scarves. Do you remember the scarf I knitted you in the last war?

Always your affectionate Childhood's Friend,

HENRIETTA

November 1, 1939

M Y DEAR ROBERT
It is really very nice to get letters from you saying you are well, comfortable, safe, and having French lessons from a beautiful countess, though it sounds rather *too* much like the lull before the storm.

French lessons from a beautiful countess

Charles says you are having a good war, and would you like to change places with him? Poor Charles! He does hate the idea of being stuck down here for the duration, saying 'There! There!' to old ladies, and still lives in hopes of being called up. Colonel Simpkins said to him yesterday, 'What? You here still? I thought you got a D.S.O. in the last war?' Charles blinked at him through his spectacles and said gently, 'Ah! But, you see, I'm too frightened to go to this one,' so we are expecting a shower of white feathers by every post.

This is a belligerent community to make up for the extreme peacefulness of our surroundings, I suppose. Yesterday was a lovely sunny afternoon, and I took Perry for a walk up the cliff path. Young Widdecombe was painting his fishing boat, and there were old ladies on seats, and a great many gloriously healthy, tough-looking babies in prams. (All the babies nowadays give you the impression that for tuppence they'd biff you one on the nose. Is this the result of Truby King methods or have they always been like this?) At the top of the cliff I had a long, earnest, nose-to-nose conversation with Mrs Savernack about the Women's Institute Choir, and on the links there was a man having a lesson from the pro to cure a nasty slice in his drive. The sea was very quiet and still, just whispering on the pebbles, and as I walked home the evening lights on the water to the west were pearly, so that I had to keep turning round to look at them. I began to wonder whether I might not be suffering from some horrid hallucination, until I saw our gas-masks on the hall table.

But in the matter of trousers, dear Robert, the war has hit us hard. Nobody can live in a seaside town without becoming more or less slack-minded. Our female visitors every summer adopt such a nautical air one expects them to break into sea-shanties any minute. But now, such is Hitler's power, this evil influence has begun to affect even the residents, and it keeps breaking out in the most unlikely quarters. Miss Piper, the girl in the greengrocer's, has gone into jodhpurs; Faith, our friend, looks quite superb in a pair of pin-striped flannels; Mrs Savernack, though I can hardly expect you to believe this, saw fit to appear last week in a pair of khaki shorts (we all consider her excuse that she is digging her way to victory a poor one); and I tell you frankly, Robert, only my love for Charles has kept me out of a pair of green corduroy dungarees.

The Linnet who looks handsome in her nurse's uniform has gone to her hospital. She writes cheerfully and says she is enjoying it so far, but oh, her poor feet!

Bill assures us that he will shortly be a real soldier.

I heard from Betsy last week. Her world has come tumbling about her ears if anybody's has, but she writes with her usual spirit to say that she is now living in the depths of the country, listening to her arteries hardening. She says she wears brogues and talks with a burr, and sometimes she wears burrs and talks with a brogue, just to make a change.

Dear Robert, our thoughts are often with you, and if I write of everyday things, it is only because I know that they are what you would rather hear about.

Always your affectionate Childhood's Friend,

HENRIETTA

November 15, 1939

M Y DEAR ROBERT
Our lovely sunny autumn days have gone, and now we have cold rain and a tearing, roaring wind. Well, let's face it: winter is in front of us now and it will be as cold and wet, dark and cheerless as it always has been.

But this winter we country people will have to try not to grumble about the weather as much as we usually do, if only for the sakes of what the papers call the Town-dwellers in our Midst. They, poor dears, are *not* used to turning a corner and being blown flat on to their faces by a S. W. gale, or running round with towels to mop up the rain and they are going to take it hard. I am sure they will need all the sympathy and encouragement we Yokels can give them.

Already it is quite pathetic to witness their dismay at the prospect of a long winter spent in Darkest Devon. 'What do you *do* in a place like this?' they wail, as they struggle back in their neat court shoes to the small furnished houses (every mod con) which they have rented for the duration of the war.

And this is where we bite back the stinging reply that there is a good lending library in the middle of the street and an equally good wool shop next door, and say tenderly that we have a Bridge Club as well as a Badminton Club, that the Dramatic Society and the Women's Institute Choir would both welcome them if they were interested in that sort of thing, and that the cinema is now open every day, instead of only three times a week, and would they care to drop in on Sunday morning after church for some sherry and meet some people?

They generally sample most of the entertainments we offer them, and I am sure they get a lot of fun out of them. You can almost *see* them at the choir practices composing funny letters to their husbands about the quaint lives we lead down here. But I am told that after an afternoon among our Tigers at the Bridge Club they grope their way home with dazed expressions on their faces.

Some of them fling themselves into the life of the place in the most astonishing manner. At the end of a fortnight they know more of what is going on than Charles and I do, and one or two of them have told us some really remarkable things about the lives of our fishermen. Charles says he is afraid the fishermen aren't always absolutely truthful.

16

Among our Tigers

We have had great A.R.P. activity in this part of the world lately. Of course it rained but in spite of that a good time was had by all, especially the fire-engine. I couldn't help feeling sorry for the 'casualties', who lay about in the gutters uncomplainingly until they were picked up. Charles, returning late in the evening, nearly ran over a figure lying at the side of the road.

'Hullo,' he said, 'what's the matter with you?' And a cheerful voice replied out of the darkness, 'I've got all my bones broken.'

Muriel is now a captain in the A.T.S. I do envy her. There's not much glamour on the home home-front. Ours not the saucy peaked cap of our untrammelled sisters. Ours rather to see that the curtains are properly drawn, and do our little bit of digging in the garden. Ours to brave the Sewing Party and painstakingly make a many-tailed bandage, and ours to fetch the groceries home in a big basket. Soon we shall have the big thrill of ration cards to add to these other excitements. And all in a Reception Area, too!

Always your affectionate Childhood's Friend,

HENRIETTA

My DEAR ROBERT

November 29, 1939

Last week I took my courage in both hands and went to the Sister Susie Sewing Bee. I have been meaning to go for a long time, but have never been able to summon the courage.

When I got to the door panic seized me, and I nearly fled, but then I remembered all that you Brave Boys are doing at the Front, and I took a big breath and turned the handle.

Who are these like nuns appearing? About fifty beautiful women, all in snowy white, are seated at three long tables, all, as they say, plying their needles. Can that be my old friend Faith, needle poised in air and a demure expression on her face? Surely, surely the Madonna at the sewing machine cannot possibly be Mrs Savernack, the Terror of the Bridge Club? What is there about a white veil tied neatly round the head that can effect this transform-ation? Should women conceal their hair? Is it a Betrayal rather than a Crowning Glory?

These thoughts surge madly through my head as I stand at the door with my mouth open. The nuns look up and then bend to their work again. I am a novice, and must be made to feel it.

Meekly I approach the High Table, murmuring, 'I've

come to sew, and I've brought my own thimble and cotton.' I hope that this miracle of forethought will commend me to authority, but the Mother Superior is unmoved.

'Have you brought your white coat and veil?' she says.

'I'm afraid I haven't.'

'You'll have to go out and buy them,' she says kindly. 'You can get some quite inexpensively at Dobson's.'

Ears red with shame, I creep out and buy a white coat and veil inexpensively at Dobson's. Then there is the horror of getting in all over again, but this time I pause to put on my armour. The looking-glass in the Ladies' Cloaks is small and spotty, but even so I can see that I am the only woman in the world who is not improved by a white veil tied round the head, and it is with almost as much trepidation as before that I make my second entrance.

But this time all is changed. I have taken my vows, and the nuns smile a welcome. Several wave, and one kisses her hand.

Greatly encouraged, I approach the High Table once more, and am given a piece of flannel to make into a hot-water-bottle cover. Now nobody enjoys a bit of herring-boning more than I, and the flannel is of a heavenly blue, so I am quite delighted with my task. But why the veil? Why the white coat? Am I dirtier than the feet of the B.E.F.?

'Fancy you being able to sew!' says one of the nuns, making room for me beside her at the table.

'Yes, and I can read and write as well,' I say. This is the sort of joke that Charles says he wishes I wouldn't make.

My neighbour is engaged upon a complicated piece of work, and is executing it with proficiency. 'What are you making?' I ask with respect, deeply conscious of my novice's task.

Sheep and Goats

'A helpless-case night-shirt,' she says briskly.

I look round. The nuns are bending over their work, and the low buzz of demure chatter fills the room. Helpless-case night-shirts, swabs, and many-tailed bandages. Young bodies maimed and broken, and dark hours of pain and despair watching for morning to lighten the windows ... It doesn't do to think too much these days, even at a Bee.

But agonizing doesn't sew a seam, and salt tears on hospital supplies would be far from aseptic. I look at the wise and busy nuns and thread my needle. This simple action is watched intently by my neighbours.

I know several things about Sewing Bees now, Robert, which I never knew before, and one is that all sewers are divided into Sheep and Goats. The Goats are the ones whose thread comes off pink at the tip when licked!

Always your affectionate Childhood's Friend,

HENRIETTA

December 6, 1939

M Y DEAR ROBERT
The Authorities are getting very dashing. Can I *really* put B.E.F. on your letters now? It all seems very reckless and risky and I only hope the Censor is not Losing Grip.

You say I never mention my children these days. Well, there's a reason for that. Nobody in the world enjoys talking about her children more than I do. I have hardly been able to listen to stories about Julia not having enough blankets in her billet, so anxious have I been to tell about the Linnet's alarm clock going off at 5.30 every morning.

And then about a fortnight ago, like a blinding light the thought came to me that if we didn't take care, this Mother-talk would soon become one of the major horrors of the home home-front and worse than the Black-out Blues.

It was after seeing two of our neighbours both reading letters from their sons aloud to each other at the same time in the middle of the High Street that I got my change of heart. Mr Perry's lead became inextricably mixed with their dogs', and while I was disentangling them I couldn't help hearing most of the letters, which were all about the heavy rain in France and

Both reading letters from their sons

would their mothers please not knit them anything at present.

It would be different if we could all produce thrillers like Muriel, whose son had to empty himself (I think that is the right expression) out of his aeroplane and came down in a parachute on to some telegraph wires, where he remained hanging for half an hour, while the villagers passed him up mugs of beer on a stick.

As told by Faith, it was an extremely good story, though I missed my bus staying to listen to it. But you can't very well dash away with your friend's son in mid-air, can you? But since then I have heard it five times; once from the hero's father, a second time from Muriel herself, twice from a grandmother (whom I was able to correct over the number of beers provided by the kindly villagers), and once from our gardener, whose sister 'obliges' Faith for two hours every morning.

So when you actually *ask* for news of my children I feel rather like a lioness who has been fed on scrambled eggs for a month and is then suddenly presented with a carcase. But it is with my newly-acquired restraint, dear Robert, that I tell you that Bill is still afraid the war will be over before he can get to it, and the Linnet comes home every Saturday and sleeps the clock round . . .

We have had a week of lovely warm weather.

Charles and I revelled in it, and so did the birds, who started a little tentative singing at dawn, as thrilling as strawberries on Christmas Day, but much sadder. It made me think of spring, and that reminded me that I hadn't planted bulbs in pots, so after breakfast I rushed off to buy some.

'What! Buying bulbs *now*?' said Mrs Savernack with relish. 'Mine are up at least half an inch!'

I wish I were the sort of woman who remembers to plant bulbs in time. I wish I were the sort of woman who

Shops Early, knows how to look up trains, and Accounts for Every Penny. I wish I were the sort of woman who sets one day aside every week for the linen cupboard, remembers people's names, never wastes the soap, and sends her luggage in advance.

I am not, but I am always your affectionate Childhood's Friend,

HENRIETTA

December 20, 1939

MY DEAR ROBERT

Digging for Freedom is not nearly as romantic as it sounds. Ever since the war, Charles and I have been worrying about a patch of No-Man's-Land at the bottom of our garden. Every time we looked at it, we felt we were betraying the Empire.

Not that Charles looked at it much. His gardening consists in refusing to talk to the gardener, and, occasionally, very occasionally, when the sun is really warm, taking his before-Sunday-lunch sherry down the garden path and saying: 'Is that an apple-tree or a pear-tree?'; and 'There seem to be a lot of weeds'; and 'Of course, I'd like to do some gardening myself, but a doctor has to think of his hands;' and finally, 'It would be much cheaper to lay it all down in asphalt.' Then he goes indoors to roast beef with a self-satisfied expression on his face as of one who has spent the morning close to Mother Earth.

I, on the other hand, take what is called an Interest in the garden. I shout at the gardener, for he is very deaf, standing for hours in a cold wind; but as he never takes any notice of what I say, I can only conclude that he doesn't hear me. I wake in the night and Worry about the Weeds and next morning attack them in a frenzy, and spend most of the afternoon trying to get my hands clean. I ask for cuttings from my friends, and sometimes steal them, and go out into the woods and stagger home with leaf-mould in a sack.

But there are times when I agree with Charles about the asphalt.

When the war started, practically everybody, in the most laudable way, rushed off and began doing the thing they hated most. Faith forced her way into the Cottage Hospital, and stayed there for nearly a fortnight, doing ward-maid's work; Mrs Savernack bought a book called *Brush Up Your French*; and Lady B, not to be outdone, bought a book called *Brush Up Your German*, which some people thought rather unpatriotic. Practically everybody who owned a car began driving somebody else's and Colonel Simpkins, as a protest against 'all this tomfoolery', took lessons in ballroom dancing.

I, of course, immediately felt it was my duty to

Took lessons in ballroom dancing

Dig, and announced my intention to the gardener in a penetrating shriek.

'Yu can dig 'un up if yu wants,' he said in a pitying way, and went on pruning the roses.

So as I had a free day on Monday, I put on a pair of Charles's shorts, took a spade in hand, and started.

The gardener was outraged at the sight of my legs, and spent quite half an hour peering at me in shocked surprise from behind the gooseberry bushes. Then he emerged and stood beside me for another half-hour watching my efforts with a superior smile. After that he went and sat in the greenhouse and had some tea out of a Thermos flask.

Bindweed is a crawling plant which has its roots in Australia.

I dug grimly for two hours, and then, quite suddenly, somebody plunged a dagger into the middle of my back. At least, that is what it felt like. I tried to straighten myself, but a scream of pain burst from my lips, and sweat broke out on my forehead. So, in a bent position, my chin bumping against my knees, I shuffled back to the house. The gardener, who was now eating a large slice of plum cake, was moved to laughter as I went by.

Charles, who like all doctors, dislikes Illness in the Home, said it served me right for digging, half naked, in an east wind, and ordered a Day in Bed.

Oh, but Robert!—what luxury is a day in bed, even with lumbago! To appreciate it to the full it is a good plan to wake up several times during the night and say to yourself: 'I haven't got to get up to-morrow morning.'

But perhaps the most exquisite moment of all is when you sink back on your pillows and listen to everybody else getting up. It is madness to spoil this enchanted hour by getting up yourself to brush your teeth. You must lie where you are, relaxed, happy, and dirty, calling weakly for your letters, the morning papers, and another hot-water bottle.

To have visitors during a Day in Bed is a grave error. It means getting out to do your hair, make up your face, and have your bed made. A little talk on the telephone with some sympathetic friend who is really interested in your symptoms is the only social intercourse that should be allowed. A good deal of pleasure can be derived from asking for your fountain-pen and notepaper, and then not writing any letters . . .

Lady B who just dropped in—a welcome visitor at any time—says she got so angry with Lord Haw-Haw the other night that she took off her shoe and threw it at the wireless, and broke a valuable vase. Now she has adopted a different technique. Before going to bed she sits down and writes a letter to Hitler, telling him just exactly what she thinks of him. She says it has never failed to give her a good night's sleep. I think her great-grandchildren will enjoy those letters, don't you?

Always your affectionate Childhood's Friend,

HENRIETTA

December 27, 1939

MY DEAR ROBERT
You know the way Faith has of suddenly producing celebrities out of a hat? Her latest is a Conductor —of singing, not trams—and the whole village has become vocal-conscious.

Snatches of song are heard on all sides. Yesterday the plumber spent two and a half hours in our bathroom, which is particularly good for sound, singing Mi-Mi-Mi-Mi-Mi on a top G instead of mending the tap in the basin, and the gardener has started Bay-Bee-Bar-Bo-Boo in an arpeggio, to lighten his hours of inactivity in the greenhouse.

It all started with carols at the vicarage. The Vicar, who pounced on Faith's Conductor like a hungry lion, gave him to understand that there was a great deal of suppressed musical talent in the village which only needed encouragement.

The encouragement turned out to be the Conductor, Faith, Lady B and myself. The vicarage drawing-room was

The Vicar pounced on Faith's Conductor

cleared for action, and the Savernacks' chauffeur was there, and the post-mistress, both looking rather self-conscious—but nobody else.

Faith, who had somehow managed to make herself look like a choir-boy, turned on her best social manner and kept up a flow of bright chatter, but after a time even her spirits began to flag, and the Vicar hurried out into the highways and byways to compel somebody to come in.

The Conductor, in the meantime, thought we had better make a start, so he handed us each a copy of a carol and said we should come in after he had counted four.

He counted four, and the only thing that happened

was a shattering boom from Lady B which shook the vases on the mantelpiece.

'Come, come, now!' said the Conductor, who was behaving with such kindness and patience that I began to be afraid he might be snatched up to heaven, 'We can do better than that. Everybody must sing. *Everybody*. Open your mouths wide, as though you were yawning. One, two, three, four—'

Everybody yawned, so we had to start again; but this time we really did sing, including the Conductor himself —and immediately the door flew open and about twelve excited villagers, who had apparently been lurking in the bushes outside, burst into the room. Almost immediately afterwards the Vicar returned with two more, and the Conductor began sorting us out.

'What do you sing?' he said to an enormous young man whose head was bobbing about just below the chandelier.

'Treble,' squeaked the young man, and the Conductor reeled as under a blow.

'And you?' he said to a small, rosy-cheeked boy.

'Bass,' he boomed, in a voice that rivalled Lady B's.

We sang and sang. Just behind me was a tenor who fluted loudly and firmly throughout the evening on one note. The Conductor, who must have been in torment, continued patient and smiling, begging us to yawn and wait for the beat. Everybody got very hot and excited and forgot all about the War, the Income Tax, Rationing, and the fact that we must shortly endanger our lives creeping home in stygian darkness. At the end cakes and tea were handed round, and it became apparent what the one-note tenor had really come for.

If I were the Minister for Propaganda, Robert— and I often feel it is a pity I am not—I would make everybody sing every day, provided, of course, that enough saint-like Conductors could be found to go round.

The other piece of fun this week was a most enjoyable rehearsal of an air-raid warning.

We were told that it would take place at 9.30 a.m. At 9.29 ½ a beaming young policeman poked his head out of the little bit of police-station window which is not covered, and spread a sheet of newspaper on the sandbags. On this he tenderly laid the siren, pressed a knob, and immediately the air was filled with what we have been taught to call an intermittent warbling note.

The result was electrical. You would have thought that siren was a herald of good tidings instead of possible death and destruction. Delighted faces appeared at every window. People in the streets were wreathed in smiles and some were doubled up with laughter. Quite a little crowd gathered in front of the police station, where the young policeman, flushed with success, changed the key, like a cinema organist with the floods on him.

Old Mrs Candy, who has been in bed for four years, appeared at the front door in her dressing-gown and was given an ovation.

I haven't seen this place so gay since the Coronation.

Always your affectionate Childhood's Friend,

HENRIETTA

MY DEAR ROBERT   January 24, 1940
    Faith took it into her head to be vaccinated last week. She has a theory that the Germans are going to drop germs on us in the spring, and wants to Be Prepared. She says that the Germans are going to fly at a great height over England and release thousands of minute parachutes laden

with bacilli. The parachutes will disintegrate in descent, so that we won't know anything has happened to us until we begin breaking out in spots!

Faith says her vaccination was a great disappointment to her. She makes no bones about her infatuation for Charles, but admits that his reactions are disappointing.

She says she went to the surgery in the evening because the light in Charles's consulting room is more becoming then. This pleased me very much, because I arranged that lighting with no little care. Doctors are gradually being laughed out of having nothing but last year's seed catalogue for their patients to read in waiting-rooms, but I still think they are inclined to overlook the fact that a woman who feels she is looking her best is much easier to deal with than one who feels she is looking her worst.

Faith says she sat down on a low stool in front of the fire and pulled her skirt up and her stocking down. In fact, she took her stocking right off, because she thinks that a stocking hanging over the edge of a shoe looks sordid.

Whatever else you may have forgotten, Robert, I am sure you have not forgotten Faith's legs. She says it was a pretty sight, and I am prepared to believe her.

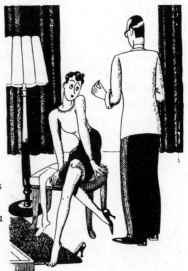

'Now, where do you want to be vaccinated?'

30

Charles, in the meantime, could be heard in the next room, madly scrubbing his hands. Then he came in with a knife in one hand and a small tube of cow-pox in the other. Faith says he was looking wildly attractive in a white coat, and she stretched out her foot to the fire and waggled her toes.

Charles came forward with his kind, encouraging smile and said: 'Now, where do you want to be vaccinated? Arm or leg?' Faith says she could have hit him. In the middle of the operation, when she said she felt faint, he said: 'Don't be so silly, Faith. Of course you don't.'

Poor Faith! I had to comfort her by telling her how Charles forgot our wedding day on Monday. As a matter of fact, I forgot myself until lunch-time, but that is between you and me ...

I have been rather bad about the war lately. This time the feelings of waste and desolation have taken the form of extreme irritability with Mrs Savernack, whom I suspect of enjoying the war because she can sit on committees and boss everybody about as much as she likes, as well as practising those small economies so dear to her heart.

Yesterday, when I was changing my book at the library, she told me, firmly and loudly, that this war was a Crusade. I said I seemed to have heard that before somewhere, about twenty years ago.

'Oh, *that* war,' she said. 'That was quite different.'

When I asked her why, she said that, for one thing, the last war had been entirely unnecessary.

Having dismissed the sacrifice of a few million young lives as a sort of boyish prank, she bought a box of rubber bands and left the shop.

Always your affectionate Childhood's Friend,

HENRIETTA

February 7, 1940

M<small>Y</small> D<small>EAR</small> R<small>OBERT</small>
Now that we may talk about the weather, I will tell you that it was very cold indeed after Christmas, and in early January. Our Visitors kept on saying, 'Do you call this Devon?'; and, really, one could hardly blame them. The fact that there were seventy-nine degrees of frost in Russia did little to cheer them, and the burden of their refrain was that they came here because they understood that it was the Riviera of the West.

It will shake you, Robert, when I tell you that there was skating on the Eel Ponds, but that is a fact. There hasn't been any skating in this place, so old Widdecombe tells me, since the year you and I had measles and missed it all.

I went down one afternoon and it was a gay sight. Not that many people were actually skating, because, of course, hardly anybody in this part of the world knows how to, even if they had skates, which they haven't. But there was a large, admiring, pink-nosed crowd watching. The sun was shining out of a perfectly clear blue sky, and I felt that if only the Visitors could have been told that this was the Switzerland of the West they might feel that they were getting their money's-worth, and stop grumbling.

Mrs Savernack, with a grim expression on her face, and wearing a peculiar woollen cap which I feel she must have bought in Switzerland a long time ago, was skating round and round the pond in an efficient way. Every now and then she would suddenly turn and begin going backwards. Each time she did this there was a murmur of applause from the crowds on the bank.

Faith, looking quite lovely in a yellow jumper, was skimming about with her Conductor, their arms linked together. 'I didn't know you could skate so well, Faith,' I said enviously when they came to rest beside me.

'My dear, I can't,' she said with a happy smile. 'I should fall *flat* on my face if he let go of me.'

But shortly afterwards, when the Conductor fell flat on his face, I saw Faith pick him up in the most efficient way, so I fancy she was not quite the novice she would have us believe. Nobody in the world can be as helpless and clinging as Faith when she wants a strong, manly arm all to herself.

Colonel Simpkins in a corner, his back very straight and his chest stuck out, was doing something clever round an orange. But he had to keep stopping to chase away little boys who wanted to slide. As a matter of fact, I was longing to slide myself, but apparently it is not done on skating ice. After a time, when his back was turned, one of the urchins stole the orange, so that was the end of all his fun, and after an unsuccessful attempt to link up with Mrs Savernack he lost heart, and began taking off his skates.

I was just beginning to think it would be nice to feel my toes again, when Lady B arrived, looking very trim in a black, pleated skirt.

'Good Lord! What have we here?' said Mrs Savernack, and Colonel Simpkins went quietly away and fetched a ladder which had been brought down in case of emergency.

Lady B was puffing a bit by the time she had laced up her boots, and I trembled for my old friend as I helped her on to the ice.

Floated away like a big, black bird

Once there, she took a few faltering steps, and then suddenly she lifted up her arms and floated away like a big, black bird. Everybody gasped. You couldn't have believed, Robert, that anything so—well—bulky could have been so light and graceful. Faith said it reminded her of those very big, black smuts which float in the air when your chimney is on fire.

'By gad! The woman can skate!' shouted Colonel Simpkins and he began tugging at his boot-laces.

Several people who had hitherto been too nervous to venture far from the edge, now struck boldly for the middle of the pond. Somebody arrived with a gramophone, and started the 'Merry Widow' waltz, and Colonel Simpkins and Lady B swooped away in each other's arms, a challenge to Old Father Time, if ever there was one.

An unfortunate girl who was due at a V.A.D. lecture thrust her skates into my hand, and, before I knew where I was, Faith and the Conductor had laced me up and supported my trembling feet on to the ice, where they each took an arm, and I immediately developed acute pain in the calves of both legs.

Mrs Phillips came down from the house and asked us all to tea. We made toast and ate it with bloater-paste to disguise the margarine, and Lady B, who was puffed but happy, told us how she had won some quite grand skating competition in Switzerland when she was young, and Colonel Simpkins said *everybody* ought to skate round an orange *always*.

As we walked home, the young moon was rising behind the trees, with one very bright star in the top left-hand corner. Mrs Savernack said it wasn't a star but a planet. I said I preferred to call it a star.

Mrs Savernack said accuracy had never been Henrietta's strong point.

Colonel Simpkins said soothingly that a rose by any other name would smell as sweet.

Always your affectionate Childhood's Friend,

HENRIETTA

MY DEAR ROBERT

A few days ago I took Mr Perry for a walk along the sea-front as far as the rocks. You couldn't call it a spring day, but it was the sort of day which makes you feel that spring may not be so very far away after all. Mr Perry, who hates the cold, was frisking along in a light-hearted manner, looking very handsome in his little coat, and a redshank on the marsh was giving its strange, questioning cry. I was just trying to decide whether it was saying 'Why?' or 'Who?' when I saw Faith rushing along the path towards me. She was gasping for breath and her face was quite white.

'What is it?' I cried.

'Mine!' gasped Faith, seizing me with both hands.

'What is yours, Faith, dear?' I said gently, for indeed, Robert, I had begun to think she had lost her reason.

'Mine, you fool!' she shouted, and with one shaking hand she pointed towards the sea. Then she pushed me aside and rushed on.

I looked where she had pointed and there, bobbing up and down not far from the shore, and drifting steadily towards the rocks, was a large, round, black object.

I stood rooted to the spot with horror, and felt the palms of my hands go damp. Nobody in the world is more frightened of being blown up than I, but there is just one thing I am more frightened of still, and that is a big BANG. To my mind, when threatened with a bang there is only one thing to do, and I did it. I sat down on the ground, put my fingers in my ears, shut my eyes tightly, and began singing the 'Pilgrims' Chorus' out of 'Tannhäuser' as loudly as I could.

Mr Perry came and sniffed delicately at my ear, and I stopped singing for one moment to say, 'Go home, Perry, darling,' and opened one corner of my eye to see him saunter off in a nonchalant manner. Then I began singing again.

How long I sat there I do not know, but it seemed

hours, and I was beginning to get very hoarse when I felt a light tap on my shoulder and opened my eyes to see Colonel Simpkins bending down and peering at me with a red, anxious face.

'My dear lady!' he said. 'Are you ill?'

Without stopping singing, I pointed at the sea. The mine was now only a few feet from the rocks.

'Good God!' said Colonel Simpkins, and then he began methodically emptying his pockets. First he took out a gold half-hunter watch, then his money, a note-case, his ration-books and his identity-card and laid them in my lap. Then he removed his Special Constable's badge and put it with the other things.

'What are you going to do?' I cried, but his reply was inaudible.

'I can't hear what you're saying!' I yelled.

'Then take your fingers out of your ears,' he shouted irritably, and began walking down the beach.

'Oh, don't do that, Colonel Simpkins!' I shrieked. 'Oh, please, please! Think of Mrs Simpkins!'

'You get down the other side of that bank and cut along,' he said kindly, and walked on.

'Oh, what a tiresome old man you are!' I cried, capering about on the bank with my fingers in my ears. How could I cut along and leave him to be blown to smithereens? And yet, on the other hand, how, oh, how could I find the courage to follow him?

Suddenly a large wave lifted the mine in the air and swept it towards the rocks. I uttered a loud scream and took a flying leap down the other side of the bank. The next thing I remember was Colonel Simpkins forcibly removing my fingers from my ears and telling me that it wasn't a mine, but a barrel.

'I rather suspected it from the first,' he said.

'Then why did you remove all your valuables?' I said crossly, helping him to pick them up, for they were scattered all over the path.

By the way, Robert, *is* there a Special Medal for Special Constables?

Always your affectionate Childhood's Friend,

HENRIETTA

'Think of Mrs Simpkins!'

M Y DEAR ROBERT
We have had a jumble sale to collect money for the Sewing B, which has sewn with such industry that it has run short of flannel. The sale was conducted with terrifying efficiency by Mrs Savernack, and enough money was raised to buy flannel for at least a million hot-water-bottle covers, not to mention shirts and pyjamas. Lady B says that had she known jumble possibilities, she'd have had one for herself years ago.

And immediately looked like a fashion-plate

We had a White Elephant Stall, too, and it did a roaring trade in Indian brass bowls, brass trays, and little brass figures of animals which people, who now have to do their own housework, have got tired of cleaning. Some of our drawing-rooms now have a sad, depleted look, but better six Polish shirts than one Benares tray, as Mrs Simpkins said bravely when she saw her favourite piece borne away by the charwoman.

Faith took a fancy to a jumble hat and insisted upon buying it. Mrs Savernack made her pay five shillings for it, though it was marked at sixpence, which I thought rather unfair, but Faith said it was cheap at the price. Lying there with the jumble it looked an awful hat, but Faith gave it a tweak and a pinch and put it on her head, and immediately looked like a fashion-plate. And some people think her stupid!

On Sunday, when I was out for a walk, a sudden gleam of sunshine on the sea made me sit down on the leeward side of the shelter to enjoy it.

In there already was a master from the preparatory school which has evacuated itself upon us, and some boys in red caps. He was reading to them out of the Sunday paper about the boarding of the *Altmark*, and if it had been a Boys' Book of Adventure it couldn't have been more exciting. When he got to the part where the sailors said, 'Are there any British down there?' and the prisoners shouted, 'Yes!' and the sailors said, 'The Navy is here,' the little boys cheered shrilly. I wanted to cheer too, but I knew it would have embarrassed them if I had. Ladies mustn't cheer, so I didn't. Then the questions began.

'They jumped down on the *Altmark*'s deck, didn't they, Sir?'

'Yes, Peter.'

'With cutlasses, Sir?'

'Probably.'

'Oh, Sir! In their teeth, Sir?'

'They might have.'

'Coo!'

'I'm going into the Navy,' said one little boy truculently.

'You'll have to work harder at your arithmetic, Colin, or you won't pass the exam,' said the master, rather brutally.

'You wanted to go into the Navy yourself, didn't you, Sir?' said Colin, pulling the master off his high horse with one fiendish tug.

'Yes. I got ploughed for my eyesight.'

'Didn't those chaps have *anything* to eat but black bread and tea, Sir?'

'Nothing.'

'And no milk or sugar in the tea, Sir?'

'No.'

'The Germans are dirty swine, aren't they, Sir?'

'Well—'

'So are the Norwegians, aren't they, Sir? Because they knew all the time our chaps were on board, didn't they, Sir?'

'Well—'

'They *are* dirty swine, aren't they, Sir?'

The master looked round the shelter like a hunted stag, and I got up and walked away. I thought he might find it easier to answer these questions if I wasn't there.

My dear Robert, had you ever thought what problems this beastly war must cause to teachers of History who love both their country and the Truth?

Always your affectionate Childhood's Friend,

HENRIETTA

March 13, 1940

My Dear Robert

This has been Marmalade Week. Every housewife in the place has been going about with a wild look in her eye and sticky fingers, and as you walked down the street a delicious smell of boiling oranges came wafting from kitchen windows.

This year, thanks to our Adolf, it is a rough-and-ready sort of brew, and my heart goes out to dear old Mrs Simpkins, whose marmalade, cut up by hand and with two pounds of sugar to every pint of pulp, used to be her pride and joy.

Faith, who must be in the mode or die, became Marmalade-Conscious for the first time in her life. Up till now, except for eating it at breakfast every morning, she has left the whole thing in the hands of her capable cook, but this year sugar became a burning question that it was impossible to ignore. She was further inspired by a picture in a sales catalogue of a particularly fetching sort of smock entitled 'When my Lady goes a-Cooking', and sent for one in powder-blue.

'I am making the marmalade myself this year,' she said nonchalantly one afternoon at the Sewing Bee.

Every woman in the room laid down her needle and said, 'How much?'

'Oh, about eighty pounds,' said Faith airily, without looking up from the rather bad herring-boning she was doing on a bed-jacket.

There was silence while people counted up the members of Faith's household and did a short sum in their heads.

'Where are you going to get the extra sugar from?' said Mrs Savernack, who always does sums quicker than anybody else.

'Aha!' said Faith roguishly.

There was a lot of ugly muttering in corners after this, and several people said that Admiral Marsdon, our Food Controller, who is one of Faith's most ardent admirers, ought to be reported to the police.

'Where *did* you get the sugar, Faith?' said Lady B as we walked home afterwards, but Faith only laughed and asked us to what she was pleased to call a Marmalade Rout on the following Thursday.

Admiral Marsdon, who hands round the bag in church, is one of those people on whose integrity one would stake one's very life; but when Lady B and I saw him walking up the drive in front of us on the day of the Marmalade Rout, we both had twinges of doubt.

'Wonderful little woman, isn't she?' he whispered to me in the hall.

'Wonderful!' I said bitterly, thinking of my meagre row of jars, and Charles, to whom marmalade is dearer than life itself.

In the kitchen we found Faith, looking quite lovely in her powder-blue smock, and the Conductor, looking fatuous. On the table was a pile of oranges which nearly reached to the ceiling, and a perfectly inadequate supply of sugar.

'Where's the rest of the sugar?' said Lady B.

'Aha!' said Faith.

'I wish you wouldn't keep saying "Aha"!' I said crossly.

'She's got some special method,' whispered the Admiral, his face alight with admiration. 'I'm here really in an official capacity—as Food Controller, you know.'

Lady B and I exchanged guilty looks. To think we had so cruelly misjudged one who hands the Bag.

'Ladies and Gentlemen,' said Faith, and the Admiral and the Conductor clapped, 'I will now disclose my method, and I really can't think why none of you thought of it before. There it is!'

With a sweeping gesture she pointed to two rows of little bottles on the dresser. Lady B picked one up and peered at it closely. Then she handed it to me in silence ... It was saccharine.

Faith was a little disappointed when we told

Stirred steadily in waltz-time

42

her that her method wouldn't work, but took it in good part, and the Marmalade Rout, which ended in making thirty pounds instead of eighty, became quite a hilarious party, with cocktails at the end. We all put on aprons and helped. The Conductor turned out to be quite a Marmalade King in his way, and stirred steadily in waltz-time to the Jewel Song from 'Faust'.

Always your affectionate Childhood's Friend,

HENRIETTA

P.S. Lady B's granddaughter Hilary is home on leave. She has become a Cook-Sergeant-Major in the V.A.D.s, and Lady B is entranced.

March 20, 1940

MY DEAR ROBERT
Whatever the meetings of our Drama Club may be, they are certainly not dull. Our club has the charming and original custom of leaving the choice of a play to the members themselves, instead of to a committee, and though this leads to a certain amount of confusion and delay, it adds a good deal to the gaiety and excitement of the members' lives; and, after all, what else is a Drama Club for?

'Now, about a play for the spring,' said the chairman.

' "Charley's Aunt",' said Colonel Simpkins loudly.

'I suggest a Noël Coward play,' said Faith, conscious that she had the clothes to carry it off. 'What about "Design for Living"?'

'It's very improper,' said Mrs Savernack.

'It's very funny,' said Faith.

43

'Whatever happens, we must keep this club *clean*,' said the Admiral, looking as he does when he stands at the end of a pew waiting for the bag to come to him.

'I always think "Private Lives" sounds a nice, homely play,' said old Mrs Simpkins. 'Not that I've seen it, of course.'

'What about "Cavalcade"?'

'Wouldn't the train be rather difficult?'

After this there was silence until a stranger got up and said, 'Mr Chairman,' in a contralto voice which commanded attention. I could only see her top half, which was hung with beads and suggested that the bottom half had a longish skirt and sandals.

'Who's that?' I whispered.

'Mrs Whinebite,' whispered Lady B. 'Taken Gorse View for six months.'

'My suggestion for the club,' said the new tenant of Gorse View, 'is "Mourning Becomes Electra".'

'Isn't it rather long?' said the Conductor, who was the only other person in the room who had ever heard of it.

'It lasts four hours,' said Mrs Whinebite.

'Good God!' said Colonel Simpkins.

'I don't think people would like missing their dinners,' said Lady B, who certainly wouldn't like missing hers.

'We might have a snack-bar,' said Faith. 'Ah, but would they let us have a licence?'

'Ladies and Gentlemen, *please*,' said the chairman. 'What is the subject of this play?' he said, turning to Mrs Whinebite.

'Incest,' she said simply.

'Oh, dear!' said Lady B.

'I will have this club kept CLEAN!' shouted the Admiral.

'If this club isn't prepared to do Good Stuff, then it isn't worth bothering about,' said Mrs Whinebite.

'If you call a lot of perverted balderdash Good Stuff, Madam, then I'm sorry for you,' said the Admiral stiffly.

'Sir! You have insulted my wife!' said a little man shrilly from the back of the hall.

Here we had the makings of a Good Row, and there is nothing our club enjoys more. Knitting was laid aside, and several people who had been asleep woke up, and said, 'What's happening?' in a pleased and excited way.

'I will have this club kept CLEAN!'

'I'm sure Admiral Marsdon intended nothing of the sort, Madam,' said the chairman but was interrupted by Mrs Whinebite and her husband leaving the hall.

I was surprised to see that she wore high-heeled shoes and a short skirt, which just shows that you can't judge people's bottom halves by their tops.

Always your affectionate Childhood's Friend,

HENRIETTA

March 27, 1940

MY DEAR ROBERT

Meat rationing is now in full swing. As a matter of fact, it has turned out to be a good deal better than we feared, but during the first week we were all convinced that we wouldn't get nearly enough to eat, and we endured

45

strange and unnecessary privations. Never having been what you might call carnivorous, it was not the smashing blow to me that it was to some, especially as I could have curried lentils and rice as often as I liked.

But Charles is one of those people who like what is called good, simple English fare, which means two nice lamb cutlets, followed by kidneys on toast, and in case the news has not reached you on your far-flung battle-line, Robert, I may as well tell you that kidneys, though not actually rationed, are more precious than rubies these days. Though he is far too noble to grumble, he does look a little wistfully at the unlikely looking dishes which are put before him.

'What is this, Henrietta?'

'Well, dear, it's a tiny teeny little bit of mutton mixed up with some spaghetti and tomatoes.'

'I see.'

Lady B, who is a wonderful cook, is perfectly happy tossing up one delicious omelette after another.

Mrs Savernack, that woman of action, took out a gun-licence. If she can't get meat at the butcher's, she will go out and shoot it. The rabbits which for years gambolled happily in the fields at the back of the Savernacks' house have received a rude awakening, and Mrs Savernack, flushed with success, has begun to turn her thoughts to bigger game. Farmer Barnes, wisely perhaps, has moved his cows to another field.

But the one who is really enjoying the meat rationing is Mrs Whinebite. Not that it actually makes any difference to her, for she and the unhappy Julius have been vegetarians of the most violent order for years, but it gives her the chance to show off in the way vegetarians are so fond of doing. She wanders about the countryside, singing folk-songs, with her hair coming down and her hands full of the most revolting fungi.

'Surely you're not going to eat those?' said Lady B, her eyes wide with horror, when we met Mrs Whinebite one day in Harper's Woods.

'Why not, dear lady?'

'Because they look poisonous to me,' said Lady B.

'They may look poisonous to you,' said Mrs Whinebite, 'but as a matter of fact they are extremely nourishing as well as delicious. Julius and I have practically lived on fungi ever since we were married, and we haven't had a doctor in the house for ten years. Not once!' she said, looking at me defiantly.

I said how nice.

'If everybody lived as we do,' said Mrs Whinebite with triumph, 'your husband wouldn't have any patients.'

I said I supposed people would still break their legs from time to time.

'Break their legs!' she said scornfully, and made a dive for a vermilion mushroom growing from the root of a dead tree.

Colonel Simpkins always does the shopping for Mrs Simpkins, and I met him yesterday on the hill with his basket.

'Do you know what I have here?' he said, holding it up and looking at me with round eyes.

'Liver,' I said.

'*Tripe*,' he said, in a low voice.

'I believe it is very good if you boil it for several days,' I said.

'Tripe,' he said

47

'But think of the gas,' said Colonel Simpkins.

'Yes, indeed,' I said.

'I must say, I never thought I'd come to tripe,' said Colonel Simpkins sadly. Then his face brightened. 'If you ask me,' he said, 'I think this rationing is simply offal.'

And I had so *hoped*, Robert, that we were going to get through our first week of meat rationing without anybody making that joke.

Always your affectionate Childhood's Friend,

HENRIETTA

P.S. A 'phone message has just come for Charles asking him to go at once to Gorse View to see Mr and Mrs Whinebite, who are suffering from gastric influenza.

Gastric Influenza!...Ha!

May 29, 1940

M Y DEAR ROBERT
It is nice to be one of those people who are told to keep in the open air as much as possible, because it gives me the best possible excuse to neglect all duties and sit on the roof, which is what I am doing now. But it's all wrong to be here alone, without the Linnet and Bill and their friends sprawled about half-naked on mattresses, and you, with your hat tilted over your eyes, sleeping like one dead, and Charles arriving in a hurry with a glass of sherry in his hand and saying, 'I never *saw* such lazy people.'

How happy we were, and how little we realized how nice it was to be lazy and happy, without fear and anxiety and horror knocking at the back of one's brain like a little gnome with a hammer.

Where are those children whose only anxiety then

48

was to get nicely browned on both sides, like a fillet of fish? And where are you, Robert? I know you aren't where you were before, but where are you?

It's not much fun, you know, being a middle-aged woman, safe and protected, on a roof, thinking of other people in danger.

You will say that this is no way to cheer a Brave Soldier—and how right you will be!

You always like to hear about this place, so I will tell you that, outwardly anyway, it is just as it always was. On each chimney-pot sits a motionless seagull. Out at sea a few people are doing a little desultory sailing and sea-fishing, and one poor brute is having trouble with his outboard motor.

Most of the bathing-huts are painted now and look very fine. Faith, of course, has out-hutted us all. A bathing-hut, to my mind, is a small wooden sentry-box crammed with damp towels, sand-shoes, black spectacles, melting chocolate, and fishing-tackle, and with so many wet bathing-dresses on the floor it is difficult to find anywhere to stand. But Faith has procured for herself a sort of mansion in off-white, with pale-green china on hooks, and a kettle, and chintz curtains with lilies of the valley all over them, and six green deck-chairs with canopies and salmon-pink cushions.

She had what she called a hut-warming on Saturday afternoon, to which she invited Lady B and me and the Conductor. Lady B and I went feeling rather sheepish, because, a you know, Robert, having tea at a bathing-hut is one of the things Old Residents just don't do; but, of course, we didn't want to miss one of Faith's parties.

Faith was looking lovely in a pair of white linen shorts, and the Conductor became quite pale with love at the sight of her. We sat on the green deck chairs with the pink cushions behind our heads, and ate asparagus wrapped up in thin slices of brown bread and butter.

'How heavenly this is!' sighed Faith.

'Perfect!' croaked the Conductor, looking at Faith as Hiawatha looked at Minnehaha, with eyes of longing.

Looking at us through field-glasses

Lady B said nothing. There was a rather strained expression on her face, and I wondered whether she minded Mrs Savernack looking at us through field-glasses from the top of the cliff.

'What I want,' said Lady B, after a long silence, 'is a gun.'

'Why, darling?' said Faith.

'To shoot German parachutists,' said Lady B loudly and fiercely.

The Conductor opened one eye. 'Did He who made the lamb make thee?' he said incredulously.

'They'll be coming down disguised as angels next,' said Faith.

'Or fairies,' said the Conductor.

'And we'll have to look inside the backs of their collars to see whether they're bogus or not,' said Faith.

'I shan't shoot to kill,' said Lady B with relish. 'I shall aim at their legs.'

Always your affectionate Childhood's Friend,

HENRIETTA

M Y DEAR ROBERT
I am afraid there has been a certain amount of what my old nanny used to call 'creating' here lately, and some of it by people who ought to know better. There was a lot of gloomy talk going on in a corner at the Bee one day, until Mrs Savernack, scarlet with rage, banged on the table with her fist until all the reels of cotton and thimbles jumped in the air.

'Will you *stop* it!' yelled Mrs Savernack.

Everybody sat in stunned silence, and after a minute Lady B stopped whirling the handle of the sewing-machine and looked up over the top of her spectacles.

'Mrs Savernack is quite right, you know,' she said in her kind, fat voice. 'Gloomy thoughts don't help the men who are fighting, and good thoughts do.

'I am a great believer in the Power of Thought,' she continued, pulling out yards of tacking thread. 'I take a big breath and shut my eyes and send great waves of hope and courage and confidence across the Channel. And what's more,' she said triumphantly, 'they get there!'

It struck me what a good idea this was, and on my way home I began sending thought-waves to you and Bill, which was a silly thing to do just then, because I walked straight into the Admiral on his bicycle and fell flat in the middle of the road.

When I opened my eyes, the Admiral was bending over me. 'It was all my fault,' I said apologetically, conscious of his distress.

But whatever the Admiral's emotions, distress was certainly not one of them, for his face was beaming. 'Lie perfectly still,' he said. 'I have sent for a stretcher.'

'But I don't need a stretcher,' I said, remembering with horror that he had been attending ambulance classes.

I tried to get up, but he held me firmly on the ground. By this time a large crowd had collected, and the Admiral,

'But I don't need a stretcher!'

with a grave face, began feeling my legs, which, to his disappointment, proved to be intact. Then two delighted young men arrived with a stretcher, a lot of splints, and a tourniquet or two.

'I don't need those!' I said wildly. 'I've grazed my hands, that's all.'

'Stop the bleeding, boys,' said the Admiral, rubbing his hands with glee, and each young man seized an arm.

Mr Bolton, my friend from the Red Lion, came running out with something in a glass. 'No stimulants,' said the Admiral sternly, and Mr Bolton, distressed by my condition, drank it himself.

Tourniquets may be a comfort if you have severed an artery, but they are nothing short of torture if you haven't.

What they missed was a nasty bump on the back of my head. When I showed it to Charles, he sent me to bed and told me to stay there two days and not read.

So, here I am.

Always your affectionate Childhood's Friend,

HENRIETTA

M Y DEAR ROBERT

It is Friday, and my day for writing to you, and so I take my pen in hand, hoping that if you do have time to think of the day of the week, you will remember that I am writing even if you aren't getting the letters. Sometimes I think of you a month or two hence, when we have won this battle, sitting down with a sigh and having about fifteen of my letters handed to you in a bunch.

It is a disconcerting thought, my dear Robert, I assure you. Fifteen letters about the trivial doings of protected people in what is called a safe area! Will you read them, or will you put them aside with a sigh as something which has become unreal?

I can hear you saying, 'Why should death and destruction be more real than people leading orderly and protected lives?'

Perhaps by then we shall have shared some of your dangers, and the substance of my letters will not be altogether trivial. Well, we are ready. There is no need for you to worry about us. I am sure there is no greater coward in the west of England than your Childhood's Friend, but I hope that if the bombs do fall I shall be able to remember that every BANG here means one less in France.

The Home Defence Corps has made all the old gentlemen here very happy. Before breakfast, on the morning after the broadcast, they began crowding into the police station, and with sheepish grins giving their wrong ages.

But we married women still feel that the part we have to play in this war is mundane, unromantic, and monotonous, and there has been some ugly muttering at the Bee, I can tell you. Mrs Savernack, in particular, has been hopping mad with fury and frustration, and was all for forming a Women's Defence Corps on her own.

Faith, who happened to be sitting next to her, and

who was sick of making button-holes anyway, was fired with enthusiasm and spent the rest of the morning designing a uniform. Lady B said she wouldn't join if it were trousers, so Faith evolved a circular green skirt to the knees, with shirt to match, and a yellow forage cap which she said would look like gorse from an aeroplane.

Mrs Savernack said she wouldn't have me as a volunteer because I would get too tired and be frightened of the BANGS. I considered this a gross libel on my character and set up a plaintive mew, but Mrs Savernack patted me kindly on the shoulder and said it was my duty to look after Charles and give him hot meals at regular intervals, because he is one of the Key Men. Then she gave me Faith's button-holes to finish.

It was decided that the corps should be called 'The Women of the West', and have two Ws entwined as a badge. But it all came to nothing, because Mr Savernack Put His Foot Down, a thing he only does on the rarest occasions, and the next day they came and took away all Mrs Savernack's sporting guns, as well as her rifle and revolver. She is more or less a broken woman now.

But the result of all this excitement was that Faith became thoroughly restless and discontented, and on Monday she went up to London to look for work. I did my best to persuade her to stay, and told her the Bee needed her, but she would go.

The Conductor is heartbroken, and is preparing to follow her, which is silly, because he has a weak chest, and has been sent down here by his doctor. Besides, we need him to play the organ in church.

I had a letter from Faith this morning. She says she has got a marvellous job as Animal A.R.P. Warden. In the event of a raid it is her duty to rush out into the street and collect all the wounded and frightened animals, and take them to headquarters.

Charles says that when you think how difficult it is to collect your own dog or cat in your own home when they aren't frightened or wounded, it seems that her task will be of little practical purpose.

I need hardly tell you, dear Robert, that the Call to fill in our Identification Cards found me without the slightest recollection of where mine was, or indeed of ever having received one. However, it came to light in my workbasket when I was looking for a button to sew on to Charles's pyjamas.

I find that I grow more and more absent-minded, and I blame the war. We are so constantly urged to concentrate on keeping Bright, Brave and Confident, that it doesn't give a woman a moment in which to realise that she hasn't put on her skirt that morning, or that she is walking down the High Street in her bedroom slippers.

With a hot-water bottle strapped to her back

But I have been Digging for Victory and Lumbago again. Lady B says I am the only person she has ever seen gardening with a hot-water bottle strapped to her back.

Always your affectionate Childhood's Friend,

HENRIETTA

June 19, 1940

MY DEAR ROBERT

I have been feeling lately that I ought to make myself some new summer nightdresses. Not that there is anything actually wrong with the ones I have now. They are very nice nightdresses — for wearing in bed, which was the purpose I had in mind when I bought them. But staying in bed all night is apparently not one of the things we are going to be allowed to do this summer, and for sitting in cellars, fire-fighting, and tackling parachutists, not to mention submarines and collapsible boats in the bay, I think something a little more substantial than triple ninon and lace is needed.

As Lady B says, it will be quite embarrassing enough to have one's old friends, such as the Admiral and the young man out of the shoe shop, administering first-aid and carrying one through the streets on a stretcher, without having to borrow a coat to hide one's shame.

When I confided these anxieties to Charles, he said, 'Quite right. What you need is some nice thick woollen pyjamas.' When I asked him whether he really fancied his wife wearing nice thick woollen pyjamas in the middle of the summer, he shuddered and said, 'God forbid!' Which just shows how unhelpful even sensible people like Charles can be at times.

Faith wrote from London that thick silk tailored ones of the night-shirt variety were considered suitable, so I bought some material.

I was engaged upon this seemly task last Thursday evening, and Charles was reading an Anthony Trollope novel as an antidote to the nine o'clock news, when the telephone rang.

I answered it, expecting the usual message about aches and pains, and heard Bill's voice.

'Everything went black,' as they say in books, but it really was Bill, and in a hurry because his train was just leaving. I rushed back and knocked over a small table with coffee cups on it.

Charles looked up with a serene Trollope-ish expression on his face and said, 'My dear girl, what are you doing?'

'Bill's back!' I said, in a high, shrill voice.

'Good,' said Charles.

'He telephoned from a station. He's not wounded. He's coming home to-morrow.'

'Good,' said Charles again, and returned to *Barchester Towers*. And you'd hardly think he had been worrying ceaselessly about a son at Dunkirk, would you? But he had.

Bill has been home four days now. The first three he spent sleeping, but on the fourth he went down the town and got his hair cut, and then came home and said he wanted to go up to the Tennis Club.

The club was looking its best. Little tables with orange table-cloths were out on the terrace. The tennis courts were sadly empty, but all the bowling greens were in use, and so were the croquet lawns for, believe me or not, Robert, we are having a Croquet Tournament.

'This,' said Bill, with a happy sigh, 'is perfect.'

We ate our tea in dreamy silence, listening to the click of croquet balls, and the shouts of them that

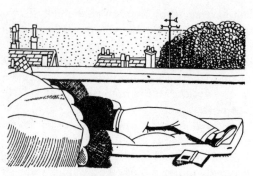

The first three he spent sleeping

triumphed on the bowling green came faintly from the other side of the hedge.

'Quite, quite perfect,' said Bill. 'Never stop playing croquet, will you? This is what we want to come back to.'

Always your affectionate Childhood's Friend,

HENRIETTA

July 3, 1940

MY DEAR ROBERT

I picked up a paper this morning, and read a cheery little article which said that if you are caught in an air raid while out in the street, the best thing to do is to throw yourself into the nearest doorway and lie on the ground with your feet towards the street, and put a piece of indiarubber between your teeth to prevent your eardrums from bursting.

I read this in a detached sort of way, and decided that I would carry a piece of indiarubber about in my pocket in case of need. And then, suddenly, the sheer incredibility of this war struck me, as it does all of us from time to time, like a blow. That we, with our electric light and wireless and Technicolor films, should have to throw ourselves into doorways with indiarubber between our teeth seemed just too madly fantastic, as well as undignified.

But now I am talking about the war, and that is what I promised you I wouldn't do, so I will tell you about the dog which has been evacuated upon Lady B. It is the size of a large rat, and has long, silky hair covering it all over, so that it is not until you look closely at it and meet a bright, knowing eye peering at you through the tangle that you know which end is which.

Lady B, whose friend did not specify the breed in the telegram announcing the animal's arrival, made up her mind it would be a Dalmatian, and was bitterly disappointed at first, but has now succumbed to the creature's undoubted charm.

'This dog is a regular Hitler!'

Its name is Fay, and though small, it is extremely fierce and autocratic, and drags Lady B about on a lead. The sight of them out together has cheered everybody up.

'Now, now,' says Lady B, 'don't drag me over.'

Yesterday she wanted to go to the shops, and Fay wanted to go to the Parade, where she puts it across big with all the local dogs. There was a long struggle, and I thought at one time that Lady B was going to be defeated, but she won in the end.

'This dog is a regular Hitler!' said Lady B.

She says that now she has Fay, she is no longer

frightened of parachute troops, and has not slept with such a sense of security since her husband died.

Always your affectionate Childhood's Friend,

HENRIETTA

July 17, 1940

MY DEAR ROBERT
However brave I try to be, and however carefully I forge myself armour to keep the Bogies at bay, there are times when it seems to disintegrate, and I suddenly find myself exposed and defenceless and drowning in dark waters. I had one of these bouts on Wednesday, and didn't enjoy it.

I was walking on the cliff path listening to the frightening noises our own soldiers make when Colonel Simpkins came up.

'Good morning, Henrietta. Have you got your gas mask?'

'No.'

'Have you got your identity card?'

'No.'

In his Special Constable's uniform, Colonel Simpkins looked at me and sighed.

'Colonel Simpkins,' I said, 'what exactly are the soldiers doing?'

'Now, there's no need for you to worry about that sort of thing,' he said soothingly, patting me on the shoulder. Then, his field glasses trained on the horizon, he went on his way.

Presently Lady B and Mrs Savernack came by and sat themselves down, one on each side of me.

'What's the matter, Henrietta?' said Mrs Savernack. 'You look like a sick monkey.'

'I think,' I said, 'that the "there-there-little-woman" attitude adopted by the Special Constables does little to inspire confidence.'

'Damned old fools!' said Mrs Savernack. 'I suppose they think we're afraid.'

'But I am afraid,' I said.

Lady B and Mrs Savernack turned blank faces towards me. '*Henrietta!*' they said in shocked tones.

'Yes, I am,' I said stubbornly. 'I wasn't afraid yesterday, and I hope I shan't be afraid to-morrow, but to-day I am paralysed with fear.'

'What you want is a drink,' said Lady B.

'Aren't you ever frightened?' I said, looking at their round, placid faces with astonishment.

'Well, yes, of course I'm frightened,' said Lady B. 'Nobody wants to be blown sky-high; but not paralysed with fear, I am glad to say.'

'If they hadn't taken away my guns, I should be *perfectly* happy,' said Mrs Savernack angrily. 'From my bedroom window I could have picked them off as they came up the beach as easy as winking. It makes me sick, it really makes me *sick!*'

'I was thinking to-day,' said Lady B dreamily, 'that if all we useless old women lined up on the beach, each of us with a large stone in her hand, we might do a lot of damage.'

'The only time I saw you try to throw a stone, Julia, it went over your shoulder behind you,' said Mrs Savernack.

'Then I would have to stand with my back towards the Germans,' said Lady B comfortably.

Mrs Savernack got up. 'Well, I must go,' she said with a sigh. 'I'm due at the Bee. But it's dull work just turning the handle of a sewing machine when you'd like to be at a machine-gun.'

'What about that drink, Henrietta?' said Lady B kindly; but I shook my head.

'You're too thin,' said Mrs Savernack, not for the first time. 'If you had some padding, your nerves would be better.'

I watched them walk away, and reflected that Charles was probably right when he said that it was the old women of Britain who will break Hitler's heart in the end.

The old women of Britain who will break Hitler's heart in the end

Always your affectionate Childhood's Friend,
HENRIETTA

July 24, 1940

My DEAR ROBERT
Our Summer Visitors are with us once more. We are resigned to them coming down every year and cluttering up the place, putting up the prices in the shops, parking their cars in front of our garden-gates, keeping us awake at nights with moonlight picnics on the beach, and wearing trousers when nature designed them for skirts.

We have even schooled ourselves to withstand, without flinching, the patronising attitude they adopt towards us—poor, simple yokels that we are.

Charles and I, every summer, even go so far as to play a game called 'Insults'. It is a simple pastime which amuses us and does the Visitors no harm. Every time we are insulted by a Visitor, separately insulted, I mean, we score a point. Charles always wins; partly because he meets so many more people than I do, and partly because his profession exposes him to insults of the juiciest variety.

They are continually saying to him: 'Can you give injections?'; or 'Have you ever heard of a drug called "M and B"?' and things like that. But somebody did once say to me, after I had recounted a modest anecdote, 'And how did *you* come to be having lunch in the Savoy Grill?'

It sometimes seems we can do nothing right.

If we are cheerful, they say: 'Of course, you people down here simply don't *realize* there is a war on.' If we show anxiety, they are moved to laughter, and say that to hear us talk anybody would think this was the one spot Hitler had his eye on. But last week, when the soldiery arrived and began their activities, a good many of them packed their boxes and went away again.

Not all, because some of them have taken furnished houses for the duration, and the relentless march of time is already beginning to change them from Visitors into Residents. Only yesterday I heard one of them say angrily: 'Really! All these strangers make shopping impossible!'

The soldiery continues its activities, and pill-boxes spring up all around us like mushrooms. Writing one's name, and a little Hitler abuse, in the concrete before it is dry has provided many of us with a lot of quiet fun, and Perry shows just what he thinks of the Nazi régime every time he passes them.

'Look!' she cried

Lady B's house is now completely surrounded by impedimenta. I met her yesterday struggling up the hill with her shopping basket. 'Look!' she cried, waving her hand towards a mass of barbed wire and concrete. 'I never thought I'd be in the front line. I'm so *proud!*'

I have been pasting strips of linen on the windows, an absorbing occupation, and one that I recommend to anybody who feels an attack of the jitters coming on.

First you make some paste according to B.B.C. instructions. That in itself induces a feeling of smug satisfaction, and tearing up material and pasting it crossways on the panes of glass completes the good work.

After putting pale-blue on the bathroom window, I was so flushed with success I started hunting all over the house for pieces of material which would tone in with the colour schemes. Yellow in the kitchen, green in my bedroom, pink in the Linnet's, it was all too fascinating, and the results exceeded my wildest dreams.

Faith, who dropped in during the afternoon and had already done her own windows expensively with adhesive-tape, stood transfixed.

'I really can't compete with that, my dear Henrietta,' she said enviously.

(But she did, because she went home and did the whole house with lingerie silk in pastel colours, each strip coming from a half-circle in the corner, like the rays of a setting sun. People go miles to see it.)

It was the duck's-egg-blue for the dining room which stumped me finally. I searched the house for something suitable, and it was a long time before I found it.

Charles, sitting down to dinner that evening, looked towards the windows and suddenly stiffened with dismay.

'Oh, Henrietta!' he said reproachfully. 'My nicest pyjamas!'

Always your affectionate Childhood's Friend,

HENRIETTA

July 31, 1940

MY DEAR ROBERT

We were all thankful when Faith gave up her job in London and came back here to be an A.R.P. warden. Partly because we felt that running out into the streets and collecting stray animals during an air raid was not suitable work for her, and partly because the Conductor, whose passion seems to continue in one long crescendo, made our lives a burden during her absence with his yearnings and lamentations.

Even Lady B and I, who are devoted to him, took to hiding behind the counters in shops when we saw him coming and putting large 'NOT AT HOME' notices on our doors whenever we were alone in our houses. Not that they kept him away, for he used to stand outside, looking wistfully in at the windows until, for very shame, we invited him in.

I knitted nearly a whole Balaclava helmet while he opened his heart to me, and Lady B said his voice was so soothing she found it almost impossible to keep her eyes open and slept solidly through most of his visits.

Slept solidly through most of his visits

One evening, when Charles had been called out to a case, I felt so sure of an impending Conductor, and so unable to cope with him, that I crept quietly up to bed at nine o'clock. I had hardly settled myself comfortably with my book when there was a timid knock, and the Conductor's face, with a distraught expression on it, peered round the door.

'You don't mind if I come in, do you, Henrietta?' he said hoarsely, and without waiting for an answer he seated himself at the foot of my bed and began—

'I don't bore you, do I?' he said about half an hour later, and I opened my eyes with a start. Lady B had been quite right about the soothing quality of his voice.

What a good plan it would be, I thought sleepily, if the Conductor could be employed as a conducer of sleep. Charles, I knew, had many patients who lay awake worrying about the war, and the Conductor was continually complaining that Faith didn't love him, because his weak chest prevented him from doing useful war work. Well then—well then—

The next thing I remembered was the Conductor's voice, still tolling like a beautiful bell, and Charles in his pyjamas standing at the door of his dressing-room.

'Hullo,' he said mildly, 'what's going on here?'

'It's Faith,' I said sleepily. 'She doesn't love him.'

'Tell me about it,' said Charles kindly, but unwisely, as he clambered into bed.

'You see, it's like this, Charles,' said the Conductor, getting off the end of my bed and transferring himself to the end of Charles's and beginning all over again.

In the morning, when we woke, he had gone ...

Always your affectionate Childhood's Friend,

HENRIETTA

August 7, 1940

M Y DEAR ROBERT

Ever since the soldiery arrived in this town a patriotic fervour has been sweeping it like a prairie fire, and everybody is getting an immense amount of fun out of it.

The Admiral appealed through a loud-speaker in the street on Saturday night for people to go and dig trenches, and there was a fine response on Sunday afternoon, and a still finer crowd to watch the fun.

The Big Moment was when Mrs Savernack arrived, in shorts, and leaping into the trench began to wield her pick with such fury that the people on either side of her moved quietly away. It warmed our hearts to see her, for she has been sadly out of sorts ever since they took away her guns and refused her for the L.D.V.

But it was the aluminium appeal which finally restored her to her old form. As soon as she heard it she rushed and borrowed a hand-cart from the Boy Scouts, and never, except possibly during the days of the Great Plague and its grisly cry of 'Bring out your dead!' have people dreaded a house-to-house collection more.

'Rat-a-tat-tat!' goes the door-knocker, worked with gusto by Mrs Savernack's strong right arm. 'Rat-a-tat-tat!' And the housewife, after peering through the curtains, runs with a smothered cry to hide her new three-decker steamer under the bed in the spare room.

'Is anybody at home?' shouts Mrs Savernack, opening the back door, and unless she gets an immediate answer she walks in and finds her way to the kitchen.

'Rat-a-tat-tat!'

'You don't want this,' she says firmly, taking a saucepan out of the cupboard.

'I do! I do!' cries the housewife, wringing her hands. 'It's what I make the coffee in!'

'You should make it in a jug,' says Mrs Savernack, and retires with her prey.

Everybody has given willingly and generously, but that is not enough for Mrs Savernack, who holds the opinion that any woman with an aluminium utensil in her house is a Fifth Columnist. After a few days her collection became so enormous she had to hire an empty shed to house her spoils, and fixed on me to guard them during her absence.

I agreed, for it is better to give in to Mrs Savernack at once, and now I spend most of the day sitting in the Aluminium Depôt worrying about the things I ought to be doing in my own home.

Did I tell you, Robert, that I am beginning to know the difference between the noise our aeroplanes make and that of the enemy?

Always your affectionate Childhood's Friend,

HENRIETTA

August 14, 1940

MY DEAR ROBERT
Do you remember Barton's Bell? It is the old ship's bell which used to ring at regular intervals during the day for the workmen to knock on and knock off their work.

Its sonorous and mellow tones were very dear to us all, and when they stopped ringing it at the beginning of the war our lives immediately became horribly disorganized. Nobody ever knows quite what the time is now, and a lot of people, who had managed quite comfortably up till then, have been forced to buy watches.

Charles says the general public nowadays is far too ready to use expressions such as 'sub-conscious', 'inferiority complex', and 'escape neurosis' without understanding their meaning, but the only way I can think of to describe what happened when Barton's Bell began ringing the other afternoon is to say that it took several minutes for the sound to penetrate from our sub-conscious to our conscious minds.

I was doing a little ironing at the time, and looked at my watch to see if it was right for six o'clock, and found it was half-past four. Then it suddenly dawned on me that I hadn't heard the Bell for about nine months.

'Parachutes!' I cried, and rushed out on to the roof expecting to see the sky full of white mushrooms with gentlemen in pale blue overalls dangling from them. It was empty.

Then for one ecstatic moment I thought the war was over, for Barton's Bell was rung hilariously in November 1918. But on second thoughts I decided that this was just wishful thinking, and that reminded me of Charles, for wishful thinking is another of the expressions which irritate him on the lips of the ignorant. So I rang him up at his surgery and asked why Barton's Bell was ringing.

'I don't know, I'm sure,' said Charles rather crossly, and rang off.

Determined not to miss any excitement which might be going, I hurried down to the end of the garden and looked over the wall just in time to see the Fire Brigade go by. After it came a crowd of people. Everybody who had a uniform, an armlet, or a badge seemed to have put it on, and was surging along the road with a do-or-die expression on his or her face.

The Home Guard was there, carrying rifles and looking happy; V.A.D.s, A.R.P.s, W.V.S.s, A.F.S.s, and a sprinkling of girl guides, boy scouts, and St John Ambulance Workers. The Transport Drivers were grinding along one behind the other in bottom gear.

'What's happening?' I shouted over the wall.

'We don't know!' they shouted back.

'Is it an Invasion, Admiral Marsdon?' I said, for I felt he would know if anybody did; but he only looked mysterious and put his finger to his lips.

Faith, lovely in her siren suit, was walking hand-in-hand with the Conductor. They looked too happy to be much use to anyone. I couldn't see Lady B anywhere, but Mrs Savernack, wearing Mr Savernack's 1915 tin-hat, was marching with the Home Guard. She had got hold of some sort of blunderbuss and was carrying herself proudly. The Home Guard looked a little uncomfortable, but none of them liked to tell her to go away.

The Home Guard looked a little uncomfortable

I watched this cavalcade out of sight, and was reflecting wistfully that I seemed to be the only person without a badge or a uniform, when Lady B came trotting round the corner, looking unusual in V.A.D. uniform and her head tied up in a towel.

'I was having a perm,' she panted, 'when the bell started, and Madame Yvonne said, "I'm afraid that is the signal for Invasion, Madam, but don't be frightened." "I'm not frightened," I said, "but get me out of this or I shall miss all the fun." '

The last person to arrive was Colonel Simpkins, in a state of exhaustion. He had been caught inspecting the defences on the beach, the wrong side of the barbed wire, and had to run a mile along the pebbles before he could get back to the parade.

In the end it turned out to be the railway embankment on fire, and the Fire Brigade, with speed and efficiency, dammed the brook and put it out. The owners of the house near by, who, fearing for their thatched roof, had not unnaturally rung up for the Fire Brigade, looked a little dazed when they saw about two hundred people and seven motor-cars pressed into the lane outside their house.

'It was the sparks we were afraid of,' they said apologetically to the silent crowd at the gate.

Perhaps next time it will be the real thing . . .

Always your affectionate Childhood's Friend,

Henrietta

August 21, 1940

My Dear Robert
There has been a sad falling-off in garden sherry-parties this year. We usually have a great many, because practically everybody here is garden-proud, and when summer comes it is their delight to give parties, in the touching belief that other people who are garden-proud too will enjoy drinking sherry and wandering up and down the paths saying 'Beautiful! Beautiful!'

Well, they probably do enjoy the sherry, but to say that they enjoy the beauties of another person's garden is just silly, because nothing fills the Garden-Proud-Person with such insane hatred and rage as witnessing results which he has been unable to achieve himself.

Colonel and Mrs Simpkins, who are as garden-proud as anybody, generally give two garden sherry-parties: one in June to admire the roses, and one in July to admire the antirrhinums. Of course, there are other flowers in their garden, but the roses and the antirrhinums are the *plats du jour*, so to speak.

One year, flushed with success, they gave two more: one in September to admire the dahlias, and one in October to admire the chrysanthemums. But there was a good deal of ill-feeling about it in the place, and, anyhow, it was cold and wet on both occasions and Mrs Simpkins caught two chills.

This year they gave the antirrhinum one only. A lot of people said they had no right to do such a thing in wartime, but Mrs Simpkins made it all right with her own conscience by having a collecting box for the Red Cross to catch the departing guests at the gate.

Charles and I enjoyed ourselves enormously, as we always do at these occasions. But then Charles and I are no gardeners; so it was with no feelings of resentment, but only those of genuine admiration, that we wandered round the Simpkins' well-groomed paths, exclaiming at the beauty of their Orange Kings, Daffodil Yellows, and Orange Princes.

'Aren't they *lovely?*' we said to Lady B, whom we found peering closely at some Fire Kings through her lorgnettes.

'It's like a seedsman's catalogue!' said Lady B, with a contemptuous snort.

Charles and I looked at each other with our eyes wide open. To have a garden like a seedsman's catalogue has always been our wildest ambition. Besides, it was the first catty thing we had ever heard Lady B say, which just shows how, far from being an ennobling pursuit, gardening simply corrodes the character.

Peering closely at some Fire Kings

After that we found the Admiral stealing cuttings in the greenhouse and discovered that Mrs Savernack has a special handbag, lined inside with mackintosh, which she always takes with her.

Feeling a little saddened, Charles and I wandered off to the vegetable garden. There is nothing in the world as soothing as a well-cared-for vegetable garden. Charles says that people with nervous breakdowns ought to take camp-stools and sit in them all day.

The Simpkins' is a particularly pleasing one, because it has flowers in it as well. Nasturtiums and Sweet Williams and Marigolds and Love-in-a-Mist—all the ordinary, cheerful, hardy flowers which nobody bothers about, and which Mrs Simpkins only picks when she is hard up for flowers for the house.

'Aren't they *lovely?*' I said to Mrs Savernack, who came down the garden path towards us, her mackintosh-lined bag bulging with loot, and a satisfied expression on her face.

'Pah!' said Mrs Savernack. 'Common annuals!'

Charles and I have decided that the only people in this place who could possibly give a really successful Garden-Proud party, at which all the guests enjoyed themselves, are ourselves. We would give it at the bottom of our garden, where the bind-weed has done so well, and there is that particularly fine bed of nettles.

Always your affectionate Childhood's Friend,

HENRIETTA

August 28, 1940

M Y DEAR ROBERT

There are sad sights to be seen on our hitherto respectable beach now that the soldiery has taken away all the bathing-huts. Umbrellas and fishing-boats are used in a pathetic attempt at preserving the decencies, but I sometimes think it would be really less embarrassing if we did without them and just undressed on the beach in a carefree manner.

I have yet to see a more remarkable sight than Mrs Savernack taking off her clothes under a large sheet with a hole in the middle for her head to poke through.

When I got down to the beach this morning, having undressed in decency and comfort in my own home, I found a large crowd watching her in fascinated silence.

'Hullo, Henrietta!' shouted Mrs Savernack, who imagined everybody was watching her because they wished they had thought of having a sheet with a hole in the middle themselves. 'Going to have a dip?'

'Yes, Mrs Savernack.'

'You ought to bring a sheet down, like I do,' said Mrs Savernack in a hearty way. 'It's absolutely splendid. Cool and cheap—and the best of it is that nobody has the slightest idea what you are doing,' and as she said this she stepped, first with one foot and then with another, out of an obvious if unseen garment.

'Yes, they have,' I said. 'I know exactly what you are doing now.'

'Don't be silly, Henrietta,' said Mrs Savernack, unfastening her stays with a loud, clicking noise. 'Now, where is my bathing dress? Just pass it to me, will you?'

I poked it under the sheet. Mrs Savernack stooped and picked it up, and after a series of contortions drew the sheet over her head and emerged ready for her swim.

When Mrs Savernack bathes she looks so like one of the comic characters out of a Noël Coward revue that it is difficult to persuade the Summer Visitors that it isn't a sort of publicity stunt. On this occasion a young man sitting near me clapped his hands and said, 'Jolly good!'

I looked at him and shook my head slightly, and his jaw dropped. 'Good Lord!' he muttered, and got up and plunged into the sea and swam a long way out, to cover his confusion.

Charles has just started his twenty-fifth series of V.A.D. lectures. All the sensible and efficient people in this place passed their V.A.D. exams ages ago, and a good many of them are already in Naval and Military Hospitals, wondering wistfully, as they clean the taps, why they bothered to learn so much about the Circulation of the Blood. This time Charles's class is composed of the leftovers, so to speak, and so you will not be surprised, dear Robert, when I tell you that I am one of them.

Not that I should ever be able to leave my home and become a V.A.D., and I feel strongly that in the case of Invasion I would be far more use running round after Charles with Something Hot in a Casserole than getting under the nurses' feet at the Cottage Hospital; but for very shame I felt I must go and swell the numbers. Besides, I rather wanted to see for myself what it is that Charles does at his lectures which makes so many ladies stop me in the street next morning and tell me that he is a Darling.

I needn't have worried about swelling the numbers, because the room, when I arrived, was packed. The class reminded me of the Middle Vth at school, which was always composed of oddities, and the girls who were too stupid to get into the Upper School. There were a lot of Visitors there as well, and a few hardened V.A.D. veterans who had passed their exams so often they thought they might as well pass them again.

I was surprised to see Mrs Savernack there, for she has always despised nursing. I went and sat next to her and she whispered to me that she was still trying to get into the Home Guard, but in the meantime she thought she might as well take the V.A.D. course. Mrs Whinebite was there, too, sitting in the front row and jangling with beads.

Charles lectured in a slow and hesitating manner, and I found it hard to believe that he had done it twenty-four times before, until I realized it was his way of getting facts into people's heads.

So many people rushed to administer First Aid ...

When we got to the Digestive System Charles displayed a fairly nauseating chart and Mrs Savernack fainted dead away.

So many people rushed to administer First Aid I thought I should be killed in the crush.

Always your affectionate Childhood's Friend,

HENRIETTA

September 4, 1940

MY DEAR ROBERT

Hoping this doesn't find you as it leaves me at present—*viz*., in prison. Well, as a matter of fact, not actually in prison, but definitely under the shadow of the Arm of the Law.

It all came of Showing a Light, a mysterious Will-o'-the-Wisp radiance which apparently shone like a searchlight straight in at the police station windows, so that the policemen who were off duty couldn't get a wink of sleep, and those who were on duty had to spend hours scouring the neighbourhood in order to locate it. But when our Nicest Policeman finally tracked it down to our house and came racing up the garden-path in full cry, it disappeared.

'You were showing a light,' he said sternly to Charles, who went down to the door in his pyjamas.

'Where?' said Charles.

'There,' said the policeman, pointing at my bedroom window.

'I don't see one,' said Charles.

'It's been put out now,' said the policeman in a disappointed voice.

The next night, just as I was doing my hair, there was another peal at the front-door bell.

'You *are* showing a light!' said the policeman, as pleased as Punch.

'Where?' said Charles.

'There,' said the policeman; but it had gone.

In the end it turned out to be the light over my dressing-table, reflecting in the glass every time I did my hair. The policeman was kind but stern about it. 'This will have to be reported, you know,' he said.

'They're getting very strict about these black-out offences,' said Mrs Savernack with relish when I told her about it. 'You'll probably have to go to Jug.'

'Darling Mother,' said Bill, who was on leave at the time, 'I will send you a doughnut, and inside will be a little file with which you will be able to saw through the bars of your cell.'

'She'd never manage it, Bill,' said the Linnet seriously. 'I shall send her some cheese crumbs so that she can make friends with a mouse.'

'The worst of going to prison,' said Lady B, 'is that you always have trouble with your passport afterwards.'

'We shall *all* be at the gates to meet you when you come out, dear,' said Mrs Simpkins, squeezing my hand.

I said I didn't mind anything as long as I was allowed to have my hot-water bottle with me, but this remark was greeted with derisive laughter.

A lot of people rang me up on the day of the trial and wished me luck. I dressed myself carefully in neat, quiet clothes, and wore clean wash-leather gloves. Charles and Bill and the Linnet said they had never seen such a respectable, law-abiding citizen. When we got to the Court they stood at the back, looking fierce and protective, and I sat myself down among the criminals.

The criminal next to me was a rather nice baby of ten

weeks with red hair. I asked its mother what it had done to break the Law, and she said it was an Angel. Then it got hiccoughs, and was turned over on to its front, and was

The criminal next to me . . .

sick on my skirt. We were busy cleaning ourselves up when the magistrates came in and everybody stood up. I looked anxiously to see what sort of an Ogre was in the Chair and found it was the Admiral, who refused to smile at me.

When you have always regarded the police as your Friends and Protectors it is a little disconcerting suddenly to find that they have become Accusing Angels. Our Nicest Policeman said his piece beautifully and was altogether fair and just, if a trifle monotonous in tone. I think that saying that a light *emanated* from my window ought to get him promotion, if nothing else does. None of the others had thought of it. But I was rather glad, as I stood there, that I had nothing bad on my conscience.

'My lord,' I said in a quavering voice, and the

Admiral looked at me as he did once at a Drama Club show when I gave him the wrong cue.

The magistrates, except for the Admiral, who remained stern, listened with compassion and sympathy to the story of the light over my dressing-table. 'One must do one's hair, mustn't one?' said a lady magistrate, and we exchanged womanly smiles. I was fined two pounds.

'You look very gay,' said the Conductor, whom we met outside our house. 'What have you been doing?'

'Mum's been up in front of the Beak,' said the Linnet.

'She had a Chink in her bedroom,' said Bill.

'Well, that's better than a Jap,' said the Conductor, who is inclined to be a little coarse sometimes.

We are still wondering why it took the police eleven months to notice that light.

Always your affectionate Childhood's Friend,

HENRIETTA

September 18, 1940

MY DEAR ROBERT
Charles said that I wouldn't allow him to enjoy the air raids in peace, and that my plaintive bleat of 'Don't-you-think-we-ought-to-go-downstairs?' was worse than the sirens. So now we have moved our beds down into the drawing-room. We took their heads and tails off them, and with nice folk-weave covers to match the ceiling they looked so attractive we wondered why we hadn't thought of divans before. Flushed with success, we sawed off their legs, and the Conductor, whose jokes have been getting worse lately, made up a new riddle, 'Why are Charles and Henrietta like their beds? Because they are low and inviting.'

So now Charles sleeps peacefully all through the night, except when patients call him out, and in the morning I tell him all about the siren and the thumps, bumps, and thuds which have kept me awake.

Personally, I am one of those who like to talk during an air raid, and make cups of tea as soon as the All Clear is sounded; and though I miss these simple pleasures there is a lot to be said for the bed-sit life which we have adopted, and Charles assures me that if the house begins falling down, a grand piano is just as good to sit under as the scullery table.

A grand piano is just as good to sit under

Did I tell you, Robert, that Mrs Savernack has startèd a corps of Women Mounties, and goes about all day in jodhpurs and an armlet. Their duties are to ride about on horseback and show people the way, like the Women Riders on Dartmoor, only, unlike them, Mrs Savernack's Women Mounties are not acknowledged by the War Office; neither (though nobody likes to tell Mrs

Savernack this) are their services in the least necessary in this part of the world.

Unfortunately, nobody here has a horse of her own except Mrs Savernack and Faith, and Faith is already an Air Raid Warden. However, now when the siren goes she rides down to the A.R.P. headquarters instead of walking, thereby combining the two jobs.

I met Mr Savernack this morning looking very worn. He says Mrs Savernack gallops about all night and only comes home when day is breaking.

Colonel Simpkins's granddaughter, Penny, who has been evacuated here from Kent, has got hold of a donkey and become Mrs Savernack's constant companion during the day. Mrs Simpkins had to put her foot down about night-riding. Mrs Savernack says she never used to have any use for girls, but Penny is different. They make a curious pair riding about together, obviously delighting in each other's company.

'Hullo,' said the Conductor jovially, when he met them this morning; 'looking for a windmill?'

'A *windmill?*' said Penny, who likes riding better than reading.

'Don't take any notice of him,' said Mrs Savernack, 'he's mad.'

The Conductor sighed. Sometimes, I am afraid, he finds us a little discouraging.

Always your affectionate Childhood's Friend,

HENRIETTA

MY DEAR ROBERT
Since the Germans began concentrating on London they seem to have forgotten this part of the world, and we feel almost ashamed of our peaceful nights. I won't say *quiet* and peaceful, because the soldiery spends most of the hours of darkness rushing madly up and down the streets on motor-bikes. Lying warm and comfortable in our beds, that makes us feel more ashamed than ever; but Charles says there is no need to worry, as we shall probably all get our turn in time.

The Linnet is on night duty at her hospital now. I asked her if she was afraid in the raids, and she said there wasn't time. The first thing she has to do when the warning goes is to chase down the corridor and persuade a shell-shocked patient to return to bed. Then she collects an armful of babies out of the maternity ward and lays them, cheeping and chirping, under the draining-board in a pantry, and after that she has to put tin basins over the patients' heads. (And if that isn't a brilliant hospital idea, Robert, I'd like to know what is.) By that time she is ready to lend a hand, in some lowly capacity, in the operating-theatre.

Faith, who must be in the mode even when it's bombs, went to London when the trouble started and came back next day looking very wan. She had thought air-raid shelters would be all song and story and *bonhomie* but found that no one even wanted to talk. They all flung themselves down on their Lie-Lows with set expressions on their faces, determined to Sleep for Victory.

Remembering the children cheered her up a bit; especially the little boy who announced, 'I like the screaming ones best,' while one was actually coming down directly overhead.

But then everybody seems to be getting terribly tough. Bill writes us the most bloodthirsty letters from the north-east coast. He used to be such a gentle boy, it is hard to believe that his letters aren't a sort of joke; but if they aren't, then he is only longing for one thing, and that is for Hitler to start invading England.

And he isn't the only one, either. It was Lady B's birthday yesterday. She won't allow anybody to buy her presents in wartime, so in the evening I took her up a bunch of roses, and found her surrounded by golden telegrams.

'Are you having a happy birthday?' I said.

'Lovely, thank you, dear,' said Lady B. 'Would you like to read my telegrams?'

I read them, and Lady B gave me a lightning word-portrait of each of the givers whom I didn't know already.

'That's Teddy Barchester. I can't think why he signed it "Edward", but they say he's grown very pompous lately. We used to know him in Rome. A very peculiar man. He used to play the violin and dance at the same time. He was very much in love with me when I was a girl.'

'Why didn't you marry him?'

'My dear! A man who danced while he played the violin! Besides,' added Lady B simply, 'he had a wife'; and added after a pause, 'she died under rather peculiar circumstances.'

'What circumstances?' I said, for this sounded as though it might be the beginning of one of Lady B's most enthralling stories; but she wouldn't say.

'I'll tell you when Teddy's dead,' she said. 'It wouldn't be fair now.'

'And who is Queenie?'

'She used to be the housemaid at my old home when I was a girl. I lent her a frock once to go to a party in, and she hooked her young man at it. She's very rich now.'

'What a lot of faithful friends you have!'

'Yes. I'm a very lucky old woman,' said Lady B sadly. I peered closely at her. Something had disturbed that lovely serenity which we all love so well. 'You aren't feeling ill, are you?' I said anxiously.

'Don't be silly, Henrietta.'

'You're not—' I hesitated, hardly daring to ask this question, for Lady B is one of those rare people who maintain that old age is not a calamity—'you're not feeling *old* by any chance?'

'Why should I feel old?' said Lady B. 'I'm only seventy-five.'

'Or frightened?'

She gave me a look of contempt, and didn't trouble to answer.

'Then what is it?'

'*Well, it's like this . . .*'

'Well, it's like this,' said Lady B, getting rather pink. 'I know it's very silly of me, Henrietta, but I did hope, I did *hope*,' she added passionately, 'that Hitler would try and invade us on my birthday.'

Always your affectionate Childhood's Friend,

HENRIETTA

October 2, 1940

M Y DEAR ROBERT
I had a letter from Dorothy Molesworth this morning. (You once played in a tennis tournament with her, do you remember?) She is working for the W.V.S. among the homeless in the East End and asks for clothes, and boots and shoes, and towels, and babies' nappies to be sent as quickly as possible.

I've been rushing round all the morning begging. I am not good at begging as a rule, but this righteous cause made me eloquent. Everybody was wonderfully generous, and I had difficulty in preventing Lady B from packing her entire wardrobe and sending it off in parcels.

In the afternoon Mrs Savernack most gallantly offered to go round collecting while I packed the things up. Of course, she went on horseback, and by the time she had tied one enormous bundle on to her back, and was balancing another on the saddle in front of her, Gertrude (which is the unbelievable name of the patient bay mare which carries her) lost patience and bucked Mrs Savernack off. Fortunately she fell head first into one of the bundles, and was none the worse.

Our biggest excitement this week, however, was provided by the Simpkinses. On Wednesday night Colonel Simpkins woke up and heard a commotion going on in his chicken-run. Convinced that it was nothing less than a descending parachutist, he rushed out in his pyjamas and found an enormous badger which had got into the hen-house through the nesting-box and was busy trying to dig its way out through the wooden floor.

There have been a lot of hen casualties here lately, and Colonel Simpkins says he was almost as excited as he would have been if he had found Hitler in the hen-house. He sat down on the lid of the nesting-box and yelled for Mrs Simpkins.

The chicken-run is a long way from the house, and Colonel Simpkins had to yell for a long time before Mrs Simpkins heard him. In the meantime the Admiral, who lives on the other side of the field, and who was just beginning to undress after duty with the Home Guard, opened the window and shouted, 'What's the matter?'

'I've got him!' yelled Colonel Simpkins.

'The deuce you have!' yelled the Admiral, who also thought it was a parachutist, and he seized his rifle and rushed for the stairs. Unfortunately, he slipped on the polished floor of the landing and fell heavily to the ground, where he lay stunned.

By this time Mrs Simpkins had woken up and poked her head out of the window. 'What is it, Alexander?' she cried.

'It's all right, my dear,' shouted the Colonel, who knows how frightened she is of walking down their drive in the dark. 'You go back to bed.'

So Mrs Simpkins went back to bed, and Colonel Simpkins went on sitting on the lid of the nesting-box while the badger scroutled madly inside and the Admiral lay unconscious at the top of the stairs.

Colonel Simpkins waited patiently for a time, but the badger became so violent he was afraid it might tear up the floor and escape, so he began yelling again.

'What *is* the matter, Alexander?' said Mrs Simpkins, leaning out of the window for the second time.

'Come down here!' yelled the Colonel.

'Oh, dear!' said poor little Mrs Simpkins. But she put on a coat and some goloshes over her bedroom slippers and crept down the drive in the dark, thereby performing an unrecorded act of heroism.

In the meantime Mrs Admiral had been roused by the Colonel's yells, and running out of her bedroom found the Admiral lying unconscious on the floor. She is a

Found the Admiral lying unconscious on the floor

woman of iron self-control, so she merely put her head in at the maid's bedroom door and said, 'Florrie, the Invasion has begun,' and then rang up Charles and the police.

I haven't space here to untangle the rest of the night's events, but eventually everyone, except the badger, was safely back in bed.

Always your affectionate Childhood's Friend,

HENRIETTA

October 9, 1940

M Y DEAR ROBERT
I visited our Cathedral City the other day with the intention of seeing the Linnet, but she never got my message, so I waited in vain outside the wool shop. Not that I minded waiting. A visit to the Cathedral City is such a nice change these days that just to watch people hurrying by with strained shopping expressions on their faces is a

thrill—even when you do it for three-quarters of an hour, first on one leg and then on the other.

I had just decided to go away, when a car stopped on the other side of the road and Hilary Dane poked her well-groomed head out of the window.

'What are you doing in our city so bright and early, Henrietta?' she said.

'What are you, Hilary, if it comes to that?' I said.

'Oh, I'm just off to my job,' said Hilary, in the fussy, important war-workers' manner which I envy so much.

'What is your job, Hilary?' I said, with all the reverence which was expected of me.

Hilary leant a little further out of the window. 'Blood,' she said in a low voice.

'Blood?' I cried. 'Whose blood?'

'Practically everybody's,' said Hilary. 'Pops Filligan and I are in it together.'

'In it?' I said faintly.

'At the hospital,' said Hilary, starting the engine. 'Come and look us up. We're slack just now. Nobody ever sees you nowadays, Henrietta.' And then she drove away.

I always get through my shopping quicker when the Linnet isn't with me, and at noon I found myself with a half-hour to spare, so I decided I would take Hilary at her word.

Hospitals always alarm and confuse me, and in spite of all sorts of notices and pointing arrows I managed to lose my way, and opened several wrong doors before I arrived at the right one.

'Come in,' said two stern voices in answer to my timid knock, and I opened the door.

'Yes?' said Pops, without looking up from the typewriter she was working with two fingers.

'Excuse me, but is this the Blood Bath?' I said.

'Henrietta!' they said, and got down from their typewriters to welcome me.

'How nice you look in your white coats,' I said, for indeed they did. 'What do you do in this little cell?'

'Blood,' they said simply.

'You keep saying Blood,' I complained. 'What do you *do* with it?'

'We group it for blood-transfusions,' said Hilary patiently. 'What group are you?'

'I don't know,' I said.

'Yes?' said Pops, without looking up

Hilary and Pops exchanged a long, meaning look. 'Are you just being your vague self, or don't you really know?' said Hilary.

'I don't know.'

'Do you mean to say you haven't been grouped?' said Pops in a shocked voice.

'Er—no. I forgot to go when they did it at our Cottage Hospital.'

'You don't mind having your finger pricked, do you?' said Hilary, who had taken some sort of weapon out of a bottle.

'I suppose you couldn't prick me somewhere else?' I asked diffidently, for I hate having anything done to my fingers.

'Certainly,' said Pops briskly as she seized me by the ear. 'You don't mind the smell of ether, do you?' she added, and began dabbing with a piece of cotton-wool.

'Not at all,' I whispered, breathing deeply and hoping I might soon become unconscious.

'Some people say it makes them feel sick,' said Hilary, who was pinching my ear. 'You seem to have very little blood, Henrietta.'

'I'm sorry.'

'Ah! here we are,' she said, and held up a small glass tube.

'It looks very pale to me,' I said anxiously.

'Don't worry, it's diluted,' said Pops with an encouraging pat. Then they smeared it on a sort of china palette and did things to it.

'Disappointing,' said Hilary. 'I thought she would be something rare and exciting.' Then they asked me my age, and whether I had asthma and malaria, and gave me a card marked 'O'. I suppose it means Ordinary.

That evening I was telling Charles all about Hilary and Pops and how wonderful they were.

'Good for them,' said Charles.

'I wish I had some war work,' I said sadly.

'You've plenty of other sort of work,' said Charles kindly; 'and what about the Bee?'

'The Bee wouldn't let me use the sewing-machine to-day. It said if everybody used the machines the work would get done too quickly.'

'I see what you mean,' said Charles.

'Everybody has a badge or a uniform except me.'

The next morning, on my plate was a little parcel, and inside a round disc which I recognized as the top of a pill-box. It hung on a green ribbon and on the disc was printed 'L.A.B.D.'.

'What does "L.A.B.D." mean, Charles?' I said, for I had recognised the printing.

'Looking After Busy Doctor,' said Charles.

Always your affectionate Childhood's Friend,

HENRIETTA

M Y DEAR ROBERT
It was a big mistake telling Faith I was frightened of bombs. Charles always says that people who say they aren't frightened are either liars or fools, so when, in the course of a conversation with Faith, I happened to mention that I hated the idea of a bomb dropping on my head, I little realized the effect it would have upon her attitude towards me.

To say it is protective is to put it mildly, and it is certainly humiliating. Twice, after air raids in the night, she has rung up just as we were dropping off to sleep again to ask how I was, and made Charles very angry indeed. If I am out for a walk with her and happen to look up into the sky at passing aeroplanes, she puts an arm round my shoulders and says: 'It's all right, Old Thing, they're ours,' and she has bought me plugs to put in my ears. But as we have no anti-aircraft guns and all our BANGS, so far, have occurred without warning, it is difficult to see how they will be of any practical value, unless I wear them all the time and carry on conversation with the help of an ear-trumpet.

If people discuss air raids in front of me, Faith makes faces at them over the top of my head and points at me in a meaning way. This used to make me angrier than anything, but now that this place has filled up with London and Surrey evacuees, each with a Bomb Story which has got to be told, I have begun to wish that I had Faith always at my elbow.

It isn't that we aren't sorry for them, for indeed, indeed we are. The first three Bomb Stories I heard moved me nearly to tears, and I lay awake all night planning how we could help them to forget. But one Bomb Story is very like another, and after a time one comes to the end of one's exclamations of horror, and the attention begins to wander. And when we try to tell them our Bomb Stories, they say 'Pshaw!' 'Pshaw!' they say, with superior smiles, and make no attempt to listen.

The person who really carries his life in his hands these days is Charles, who, when he is called out in the small hours, is not allowed any lights at all on his car, and has to steer a hopeful, zigzag course between the pill-boxes and various obstructions which have been put up all over the roads.

When he consulted the police on this ruling they said tersely that if they caught him driving without lights they would summons him. But if he drives *with* lights the soldiery will shoot him. It seems that the wisest course would be to defy the police and pander to the soldiery, only if he does that he is practically sure to crash his car and kill himself that way. So you see he is what you might call awkwardly placed.

'That raid was soon over, wasn't it?'

The Admiral tells me that we are going to have a new and much louder siren, which is a pity, because I am sure it will make everybody much more frightened of air raids. The one we have now is the sweetest little thing. Nobody hears it except those who, like ourselves, live near to the police station, and even I missed its gentle wheezings this afternoon, because I happened to be boiling a kettle at the time.

Faith, who dropped in on her way home from the A.R.P. Headquarters, found me having tea in the kitchen and reading *The Last Chronicles of Barset*.

'That raid was soon over, wasn't it?' she said in the bright A.R.P. manner they have been taught to adopt towards nervous civilians.

'What raid?' I said.

That rather took the wind out of her sails but a nice cup of tea and the cheering thought that I might be going deaf with age revived her in no time.

Always your affectionate Childhood's Friend,

HENRIETTA

November 13, 1940

MY DEAR ROBERT
It is such a beautiful day, and I am writing this sitting in the sun on my roof, which is not bad for the beginning of November. There is a soft haze over the sea, which is very still, because we have an off-shore wind. Every now and then a yellow leaf comes fluttering down from the mulberry-tree, and there is a smell of bonfires in the air which would fill me with a delicious autumn melancholy if it wasn't for the feeling that I ought to be in a London air-raid shelter, being bombed.

The fact that I am more useful where I am is small comfort. I think everybody down here feels the same way, and the corroding thought that we are not bearing our share of the burden grows and grows and is getting us all down. This melancholy state of mind is not helped in any way by our evacuees from London, who seem to be incensed by the fact that nobody in this place has been killed by enemy action so far.

We are very, very sorry for the Londoners in our midst, Robert, but we do wish that they wouldn't begin *all* their sentences with 'You people down here—'.

'You people down here make me wild,' said a London Lady to whom we had been listening meekly for half an hour at the Bee yesterday morning. 'You aren't at grips with reality at all. You simply don't *realize* what it is like in London.'

'We probably realize more than you think,' said Lady B, in her kind way. 'And anyway, why be cross with us? You might as well be angry with somebody because he hasn't had appendicitis.'

'You go to bed and sleep peacefully all night,' said the London Lady indignantly.

'We'd gladly stay awake if it did any good,' said Lady B.

'What's that about sleeping peacefully in bed all night?' said Mrs Savernack, who had just looked in on her way home after her usual patrol. 'I haven't had a night in bed for six weeks.'

'Indeed?' said the London Lady. 'And what do you do?'

'I patrol the moor on horseback,' said Mrs Savernack, 'protecting people like you. And so do the Home Guard, and the Special Constables, and the Coast Watchers, and the Soldiers, only they have to do it on their feet.'

Like the hosts of Tuscany, we could scarce forbear to cheer, for we felt that a blow had been struck in our defence.

'Pooh!' said the London Lady. 'Protecting us from what? Now, in London—'

'Don't!' said Faith earnestly. 'Don't start all over again.'

The London Lady was incensed. She rose majestically and put her thimble away in her bag. 'What this place needs is a few bombs,' she said.

'We've had quite a lot of BANGS,' said Lady B soothingly, 'and perhaps we shall get some right on the houses soon. If the Invasion comes we certainly will.'

'There's no fear of Invasion now, is there?' said the London Lady, a trifle anxiously.

'Well, you never know,' said Lady B, with an innocent expression on her face. 'The soldiers seem to think there is still some danger of it, now the nights are getting longer. They say this beach is particularly suitable for landing tanks on,' she added chattily. 'Of course, the houses on the Front would suffer most, especially the hotels, because they are such wonderful targets.'

'Lady B,' I said severely, after the London Lady had hurried away, 'I think you've been naughty.'

'I fear so, I fear so,' said Lady B contritely. 'But I was sorely tried.'

The people I really am sorry for are the not-so-well-to-do evacuees, who are crowded into small houses with their children, and I really do think something ought to be done about them. So much is done for the soldiers in the way of canteens and entertainment, but nobody seems to think that these poor women might be glad of an afternoon's fun occasionally, or that they and their hostesses might be glad to get away from each other from time to time.

The other day the lease of the cinema at our public hall came to an end, and in the middle of the night an Idea came to me about it, and I got so worked up I couldn't go to sleep again. In the morning I rushed round to see the

Admiral at the council offices, and found him sitting at a table, looking severe.

'Take that Bench expression off your face,' I said breathlessly. 'I've got an idea. It's about the public hall. Listen: the council must take it over and turn it into a People's Palace.'

Sitting at a table, looking severe

'Sounds a bit Bolshie to me,' said the Admiral.

'Somewhere for the evacuated mothers to go to, where they could have tea and listen to the wireless, and games for the children — and the Drama Club and the W.I. and all that, of course — and dances for the soldiers — and lectures, perhaps — no class distinctions, just anybody who wants to join — and a children's library — and roller-skating — and the cinema twice a week — and the Ladies' Orchestra — all the entertainments gathered into one place — the great Beating Heart of the town —' I paused for breath.

'You do have the strangest ideas, Henrietta,' said the Admiral. 'Who's going to run this Beating Heart? And, anyhow, another cinema company has taken the hall, so that's that.'

I went home feeling like a barrage balloon that somebody has playfully spiked with a bayonet.

Always your affectionate Childhood's Friend,

HENRIETTA

P.S. We had a sou'-westerly storm last week and the waves playfully pushed back some of the barbed wire on the beach into a sad, tangled loop. This delighted the fishermen, who derive much pleasure from the havoc wrought by the storms as long as it isn't to their boats and nets.

November 20, 1940

MY DEAR ROBERT

Charles's Cheese arrived this morning, and we realized with a shock that Christmas is almost upon us. Charles's Cheese is an enormous Stilton which arrives with delightful regularity at this time every year, the gift of a Grateful Patient. Charles unpacks it reverently and lifts it out of the box, murmuring humbly, 'I don't deserve it. I don't deserve it.' It is then cut in half, and one half is wrapped neatly in a table-napkin and the other half put away. One year we gave the second half to the Savernacks, on the understanding that later in the year they also would buy a Stilton cheese and give us their second half, but they forgot to do this, so we didn't try it again.

My grandfather used to bury his Stilton cheeses in the garden, digging them up from time to time in order to pour bottles of port wine into them. Alas! Those spacious days are gone. But I rather suspect Charles of ministering to his Christmas Stilton occasionally with a modest glass of something, though he is very secretive about it.

From Christmas onward, housekeeping is greatly simplified, because, whenever I say to Charles, 'What would you like for lunch?' he replies simply, 'My Cheese.'

Every day it is put on the table in front of him, and he digs at it tenderly with a little scoop. I shall never forget the day Faith dropped in for lunch and poked a great hole in the bottom of it. I thought Charles was going to faint.

And digs at it tenderly

'Christmas is nearly here,' I said, when we met at Faith's for a glass of sherry after Church. 'Charles has got his Cheese.'

'Good gracious!' said Lady B.

'I sort of feel we ought to do something about a party for evacuees,' I said, hoping this didn't sound as priggish to them as it did to me.

'Or the soldiers,' said Faith. 'I was talking to one yesterday, a most cultured man. He plays in the Philharmonic Orchestra. He says he is simply *starved* for music.'

'What's that?' said the Conductor, like a war-horse sniffing blood.

'He said there were lots of them who would give

anything even to hear some good gramophone records,' said Faith.

'I have records of all the operas,' said the Conductor, looking round happily, 'and the Vicar would lend us the church hall.'

So the party was arranged, and Faith said she would get in touch with the Philharmonic Corporal. Lady B and I used up our margarine rations making mince-pies, and even then there didn't seem to be enough, so we bought cakes as well. We managed to get hold of some holly and a little mistletoe, and Lady B brought all her drawing-room cushions, because, as she said, chairs are hard and operas long. The Conductor brought his gramophone, which is one of the superior ones which change their own records, and it was put in a prominent position on the platform. By the time we had finished, it all looked very cosy and Christmasy. At the last minute, Faith got in a panic and rushed out and bought a lot of sausage rolls. Then we sat down to wait.

We waited for half an hour, and then we each had a glass of beer and I sang them 'Sarah Jane's Tea-party', about the guests who never came. (Do you remember Nanny singing it, Robert?) It didn't go over big in any way, and the Conductor said I was pinching my top notes.

We waited another quarter of an hour, and Faith said for the hundredth time that the Philharmonic Corporal had seemed so pleased and had told her to expect a big crowd.

At the end of another quarter of an hour Faith and the Conductor got into their cars and used up a month's petrol going round collecting Evacuated Mothers and bringing them to the hall.

The Evacuated Mothers sat around and told each other Bomb Stories while the Conductor played 'Madam Butterfly' on the gramophone.

The party didn't seem to be going too well, so I slipped out and ran home to get some of the Linnet's low-brow records. When I got back the last Evacuated Mother had arrived with a soldier husband, a saucy sort of man who paid Faith compliments, and announced that there were too many ladies at the party, and what it needed was a few gentlemen.

Then he slipped away with a roguish wink and returned, like the spirit in the Bible, with seven others worse than himself, who must have been lurking outside the door.

I don't know whether it was the gentlemen or the Bing Crosby records, but the party now began to go with a bang, and ended with Musical Chairs and Postman's Knock. Every scrap of food was eaten, and the Evacuated Mothers said they hadn't enjoyed themselves so much since they left London.

When they had all gone, and we were sweeping up the crumbs, a little bespectacled face peered round the door. It was the Philharmonic Corporal. It seemed that he had forgotten to tell his friends about the party. We left him playing 'Rosenkavalier' to himself in the dark.

Always your affectionate Childhood's Friend,

HENRIETTA

December 25, 1940

MY DEAR ROBERT
A-Merry-Christmas-and-a-Happy-New-Year!   I have wished you that for so many years that I am not going to let Hitler stop me now, even though this Christmas will not be a particularly merry one, and happiness in the New Year is uncertain, to say the least of it.

When we were children and made our own cards, I remember that Mother always made us put 'Peaceful' instead of 'Merry' to anyone who had suffered a bereavement.

Well, this year our Christmas here might be better described as Peaceful than Merry in that there was no organized gaiety. Neither Bill nor Linnet managed to get home.

We had a chicken, and Lady B came to share it with us. We decided beforehand that we wouldn't try to be too gay, because if we did, we would all end by being depressed. But Lady B arrived with an encouraging-looking bottle, and Charles, unexpectedly, clambered into a dinner jacket, and they both looked so smart that I rushed upstairs, and, flinging off my sober semi, changed into the new evening dress I had bought just before the war.

I hadn't been able to resist some Merrie Yuletide table decorations, and the last of the green candles were on the table drawn up cosily in front of the fire.

Pop! went Lady B's bottle, and suddenly it became a carefree and entirely enjoyable Christmas party.

'I wish we had some crackers,' said Lady B, and I dived into a cupboard and produced a box of last year's. We pulled the crackers, and put on the paper-caps, and blew the whistles, and read each other the mottoes.

'Who says poetry is dead?'

'Sweet is sugar in my tea,
Sweet is sunlight on the sea,
Sweet is blossom on the tree,
But sweeter far are you to me,'

read Lady B with feeling.

'Who says poetry is dead?' said Charles.

Suddenly the gaiety ran out of the soles of my shoes, leaving me staring horror-stricken at Lady B and Charles, who were lighting a circular piece of paper in the fond hope that it would afterwards float in the air.

'What's the matter, Henrietta?' said Charles, looking up. 'Have you got a pain?'

'No,' I said. 'But it's awful the way we are enjoying ourselves like this.'

Lady B put her hand on mine. 'You know, Henrietta, darling,' she said, 'I think you are getting to be just the teeniest bit morbid about enjoying yourself.'

'Yes, but—' I said.

'Dost think that because thou art virtuous there shall be no cakes and ale?' said Charles recklessly.

'Yes, but—'

'It isn't as if it had cost anything except the chicken,' said Lady B. 'All the rest was pre-war stock.'

'Yes, but—' I said.

'If it's the evacuees you're thinking of,' said Charles, 'I don't suppose anybody does more for them than I do, and I don't get paid for most of it. I think I *deserve* a party.'

'Besides, it's fun to snatch a bit of enjoyment under Hitler's nose,' said Lady B.

'So don't be an ass, my darling,' said Charles, producing some port that he must have decanted on the sly. 'Get Evensong to come in, and we'll drink the King's Health.'

I went and fetched Evensong from the kitchen, and

Charles handed her a glass. 'The King!' said Charles.

'God bless him!' said Evensong.

'And the Queen,' said Lady B.

'God bless her!' said Evensong.

'Absent Friends,' said Charles. I caught his eye and knew he was thinking, as I was, of Bill and Linnet.

'And the British people,' said Lady B, while a big tear rolled down her cheek.

'God bless 'em!' said Evensong loudly, and threw her glass into the fireplace, where it broke to pieces.

'Good gracious!' said Charles.

'I beg your pardon, Madam,' said Evensong, 'but I really couldn't help meself.'

Always your affectionate Childhood's Friend,

HENRIETTA

January 15, 1941

MY DEAR ROBERT

Everybody is feeling rather flat and low after the strenuous holiday season we have had. Not that anybody actually enjoyed it, but it kept us too busy and exhausted to think, and that is a good thing these days.

Yesterday Faith walked into Lady B's drawing-room, where she and I were enjoying a little quiet knitting, and plumped down into a chair.

'What's the matter with you?' said Lady B, looking up over the top of her spectacles.

'I'm depressed,' said Faith.

'Good gracious!' said Lady B. 'Don't let Hitler hear you saying things like that.'

'Well, I *am* depressed,' said Faith. 'It's so dark in the mornings, and if you like the idea of pink brushed-wool stockings, I don't.'

'What's the matter with you?' said Lady B

'They aren't going to be pink brushed-wool,' said
Lady B soothingly. 'They'll be something snappy in lisle.
And anyhow, with your legs, my dear Faith, you have
nothing to fear.'

'Soon there won't be any face-powder,' said Faith,
who was determined to have her grumble out, 'and now
they aren't going to sound our siren any more.'

'*Aren't going to sound the siren any more?*' said Lady B
and I, laying down our knitting, for this was a matter of
deep interest. 'Why?'

'They say it frightens the old ladies.'

'Well, I *am* sorry,' said Lady B. 'I was getting quite
fond of it.'

'They're going to sound it if bombs are dropping,'
said Faith.

'Surely that will be hardly necessary?'

'The Bomb Snobs will despise us more than ever,'
said Faith gloomily.

'You should talk to them about the invasion in the
spring,' I said. 'I always do. Charles says he talks about the

barrage on the Somme in the last war, and they hate it.'

'It is only lately,' said Lady B, 'that I have realized what extraordinary restraint the people who fought in the Great War have shown all these years.'

'It's because they were men,' said Faith, who prefers the opposite sex to her own.

'About your depression, Faith, dear,' said Lady B, tactfully changing the subject. 'I suggest that you paint the stairs or turn out a cupboard. It's an almost certain cure.'

'I think I'd sooner paint the stairs than turn out a cupboard,' said Faith doubtfully, and soon afterwards she and I took our leave.

On the way home Faith and I had the delightful and almost unique experience of knocking on the door of the police station and telling them they were showing a chink of light. This threw Faith into the highest good humour, ańwhen I left her at her gate the black cloud had lifted and I could see she had forgotten it had ever been there.

Always your affectionate Childhood's Friend,

HENRIETTA

M Y DEAR ROBERT   January 22, 1941
Evensong* says that now 'Awfuls' are rationed we shall have to put our Thinking Caps on when ordering the meals. Personally, I have always had to put my Thinking Cap on when ordering meals, even in the days of plenty, and I don't consider the morning's agony in the kitchen any worse now than it was then. In some ways it is better. What housewife has not felt shame when, with the foodstuffs of the world at her disposal, she has, after ten

minutes' deep thought, said, 'And then, I think, we'll have a rice pudding'?

To-day the daily ordering of meals has become a sort of game, in which the Housewife makes the moves and the Cook says 'Check!'

HOUSEWIFE: And afterwards we will have pancakes.

COOK (*triumphantly*): No lemons, Madam!

H.W.: Then we'll have apple fritters.

COOK: I'm afraid I couldn't spare an egg for the batter, Madam.

. . . has become a sort of game

H.W.: What about a macaroni cheese?

COOK (*with glee*): There's not a bit of cheese in the place!

H.W. (*warming up*): Sardines on toast.

COOK (*smugly*): Well, Madam, we've got some, but we *have* been asked not to open tinned foods, haven't we? Of course, if you really *want* sardines—

---

* 'Evensong' was one of Henrietta's two dailies. The other was 'Matins'. They did not like each other and, as one can guess from their names, it was hoped that their paths would seldom cross.

H.W.: No, no. We won't have sardines. What about a plum duff?

COOK *(sarcastically)*: Of course, if you don't mind having it without any currants—

H.W. *(loudly)*: Then we'll have a Nice Rice Pudding.

This is the K.O. for Cook, who retires muttering.

They say that oatmeal is to become our staple diet from now onwards. Charles, who has never allowed a spoonful of porridge to pass his lips, received the news without enthusiasm.

How do your hardships compare with ours? I hope I may never know.

Always your affectionate Childhood's Friend,

HENRIETTA

January 29, 1941

MY DEAR ROBERT

I have got a croaking sort of cold and am having a day in bed.

This, as you know, is a tremendous treat.

All the morning pale yellow sunshine poured in through one window, and in the evening bright golden sunshine poured in through another. The sea was a delicate mother-of-pearl colour, the birds were practising a few simple singing exercises for the spring, Perry was asleep under the eiderdown, and I had a nice book about the spacious days of Queen Victoria to read.

Now a ridiculous round, red sun has sunk into the sea, a few late seagulls have flown across the green sky to their dormitory on the cliffs, an entirely undeserved day of enjoyment has come to an end, and it is time for the blackout.

Sometimes I think the lookers-on have the best of it, and to get the full savour out of life one should take firmly to the sofa early in youth and stay there, like Jane Austen.

Have I told you I am getting worried about Perry's food. Even a little dog like him needs some raw meat occasionally, and he breaks out into a sort of reproachful eczema if he doesn't get it. Now there is talk of dog-biscuits running short, and Charles is beginning to drop hints about Perry being a very old dog and having had a very happy life, and what a shame it would be to keep him alive if he weren't healthy; and the fear, which has been lurking at the back of my mind for weeks, draws another step nearer.

I don't quite know why we are all so devoted to Perry. If ever there was a selfish, self-centred dog, it is he. Neatly upholstered, as Faith says, in black satin, and with little tan gloves on each paw, he is pleasing to the eye, but there is little real St Bernard-like nobility about him. In return for our devotion he gives us a grudging affection,

There is little real St Bernard-like nobility about him

and though there is a legendary belief in the family that he is fond of me, I know it is only because I devote my life to his comforts. Aloof and snubbing to our friends, he occasionally fawns upon people we dislike, and he has a disturbing habit of suddenly barking shrilly at nothing, and making us all jump. He has an unaccountable phobia about being trodden upon, and if you so much as touch him with your foot he screams loudly and rushes into a corner, giving any strangers who happen to be present the impression that we are in the habit of kicking him across the room. A firm believer in warmth and a hater of fresh air, he sleeps, winter and summer, with a rug over his head. Fires are lit for him, windows are shut for him, doors are opened to let him in, and then, almost at once, opened again to let him out.

'What fools you do make of yourselves over that dog!' say our guests with scorn.

'Perry?' we say nonchalantly, trying to hide the fact that we are deeply wounded by this remark. 'Oh, he's a great character.'

'Personally, I only like *big* dogs,' says the guest. 'Alsatians, and so on.' And in about twenty-four hours Perry has another willing slave opening and shutting doors for him, giving up the best chair to him, trying to pat him (a thing Perry never allows), and holding him up at the window to bark at the pussies.

Yesterday I met Mrs Savernack on the cliff path with her Spaniel, her Dachshund, her Cairn, and her Dalmatian. Mrs Savernack herself was not looking well. She gave up her meat ration to the dogs months ago, and just lately has been giving them her butter and margarine as well. Mr Savernack says he and the servants have to keep their rations under lock and key. The dogs, I thought, were looking pretty fit.

'How are you managing about Perry's food?' she said.

'Oh, we just order a dead horse for him every week,' I said brightly.

'I'm glad you can joke about it, Henrietta,' she said, looking at me with cold dislike.

'Come home and have some tea,' I said, for I felt sorry for her. 'We've still got a little butter.'

Mrs Savernack brightened visibly. '*Have* you?' she said. 'Justinian would love a little butter.'

'I'm not offering butter to your Dalmatian,' I said, 'or to any of your dogs. In fact, I think we'll park them at your house on the way home.'

Mrs Savernack sighed, but showed no fight. It was sad to see her so unlike herself.

A little farther on we found some scribbling in chalk on the asphalt path, and paused to look at it,—a nice robust Union Jack with 'hooray for good old England!!!' in chunky letters underneath.

That set us both up, and we had quite a jolly tea, but I had to stop Mrs Savernack smuggling a small piece of cherry cake home for Muriel, the Dachshund.

Always your affectionate Childhood's Friend,

HENRIETTA

February 12, 1941

M Y DEAR ROBERT
We are going to keep five hens. This news will surprise you a good deal, knowing as you do Charles's peculiar phobia about touching birds of any kind, and my deep affection for ducks.

The desperate venture has been forced upon us by our newly-acquired lodger, who used to be a fellow art-student of mine somewhere about the Regency period, and has come to live in our attics.

She used to live in Birmingham, and when she wrote to say that she found the air-raid shelter lonely now her husband had joined the R.A.F., and shopping was difficult as there always seemed to be a time-bomb outside the grocer's, Charles and I looked at each other and said, 'The attics.'

You see, we have felt for some time that we ought to offer our attics to the Bombed, but she is practically the only person we know who is small enough to stand upright in them without bumping the head. We wrote a tentative invitation, received an ecstatic telegram in reply, and shortly afterwards the lodger arrived with a vanful of furniture.

And there she is, living a secret, mouse-like life, cooking on an electric griller, and creeping down between Matins's exit and Evensong's entrance to wash a few tiny dishes in our sink. She has the same passion for privacy as I have, and we bow gravely to each other when we meet on the stairs, and only visit each other after receiving written invitations.

I must say I enjoy visiting the lodger. There is something very piquant about sitting comfortably and romantically in what used to be your box-room. The electric radiator (installed by lodger) gives out a fierce heat very much to my liking, and we talk of the old days when we used to go about dirty and untidy because we felt that otherwise we would never make our mark in the world of Art.

The only flaw in this admirable arrangement is that the woman insists upon being grateful. Why? She has made our attics look lovely, and is prepared to cope with incendiary bombs, so surely it is we who should be grateful to her.

And that brings me to the hens, for it is the lodger who is going to keep them. She seemed to want to do something to help us and impede Hitler, so we gave her the Bad Bit at the bottom of the garden. The gardener was annoyed, of course, as gardeners always are, and said he was about to dig it up for potatoes, but as he has been saying that for years, we didn't take any notice, and any morning now the lodger

Staggering down the garden path

can be seen staggering down the garden path with a hoe several sizes too large for her, and a few days ago she came to us with a light in her eye and said, 'Hens.'

'I hate hens,' said Charles hysterically. 'I can't bear touching them!'

'You won't have to touch them,' said the lodger, with a steely look; 'and you know you like an egg for your breakfast.'

'Who's going to shut them up at night?' said Charles.

'We'll take it in turns,' I said, being definitely in the hen camp and burning to give them our scraps.

'And supposing you have one of your coughs?' said Charles fretfully.

'Then *I* shall shut them up *every* night,' said the lodger.

'Well, if you must, you must,' said Charles, 'but I intend to offer nothing but destructive criticism.'

This is as far as we have got up till now:

One roll of wire-netting,
   obtained with incredible difficulty.
One old hen-house,
   obtained with less difficulty from Faith's loft.
Destructive criticism from Charles.
Still more destructive criticism from the gardener,
   who is incensed because the lodger has succeeded
   in clearing quite a large patch of bindweed from
   the bottom of the garden.
Advice from Matins,
   who says hens like their scraps hot.
Advice from Evensong,
   who says they like them cold.

One old hen-house

Advice from Colonel Simpkins,
   who says we must get a government grant for their
   food, but fails to specify how.
Advice from Lady B.
   'My dear, *don't*. They darken your whole life.'
Advice from Mrs Savernack.

'Five? Good heavens! I keep fifty!' (But she doesn't look after them herself.)

I keep on being sorry for the Evacuated Mothers—all this winter with no excitement. More and more of them keep on arriving, and you hear nothing but cockney in the street nowadays.

When Charles came in last night, hung his hat up in the hall, and said, 'How be yu, my dear? Pretty peart, seemingly?' it was like music in my ears.

'Charles,' I said, 'what has happened to the Devonians?'

'Cowering in their homes, probably,' said Charles.

'Nonsense,' I said. 'It takes more than a few hundred Londoners to make Devonians cower.'

'Assimilated, perhaps,' said Charles.

'Speaking as one Devonian to another, now *is* that likely?'

Charles thought for a moment. 'Perhaps they persuade the evacuees to go out and do their shopping for them,' he said.

'Ah,' I said. 'Now you're talking.'

Always your affectionate Childhood's Friend,

HENRIETTA

February 19, 1941

My Dear Robert
Lady B was perfectly right when she said that hens darken your whole life. They began darkening ours before they even arrived, and the first shadow which fell across our path was a nasty little buff Form. Now, there is something about a Form, no matter what colour, which renders me incapable of answering the simplest questions.

'Charles,' I said brightly at breakfast, 'here's a little Form to fill in about the hens.'

'Those beastly hens!' said Charles bitterly.

'It's quite a small Form, Charles.'

'I'm a very busy man!' said Charles, and cramming his hat on to his head he rushed from the house.

I mounted the stairs to the attics and knocked politely on the lodger's door.

'They've sent a Form to fill in about food for *Les Girls*,' I said.

The lodger turned pale. 'Oh, Henrietta!' she said, 'I can't fill in Forms.'

'Nor can I,' I said sadly. 'You know, there are times when I feel that our Art School training didn't fit us for the Battle of Life.'

In the end I took it to Mrs Savernack, who is always pleased by the exhibition of inefficiency in others, and therefore willing to help. 'Good heavens, Henrietta!' she said. 'What a fuss you are making about your five miserable hens! It's perfectly simple. Now ... How many hens did you keep last year?'

'None,' I said, and Mrs Savernack gave me a Look and wrote down five.

'Now, let me see,' went on Mrs Savernack rapidly. 'Four ounces per bird per day, that's twenty ounces a day. Multiply by thirty for the month. Twenty times thirty?'

'Er—' I said.

'Six hundred,' said Mrs Savernack. 'Divide by sixteen to make it into pounds. Quick, Henrietta!'

'Have you got a pencil?' I said wildly.

'Thirty-seven and eight over,' said Mrs Savernack, writing it down. 'Now you sign your name here. I suppose you can sign your name? That's right. Now, all you've got to do is to post it.'

'I'll just run home and get a stamp and an envelope,'

'Divide by sixteen—quick, Henrietta!'

I said, in what I hoped was a bustling and efficient manner.

'You don't need a stamp or an envelope,' said Mrs Savernack patiently. 'You just fold it up and put it in the letter-box.'

On my way home I met the lodger coming out of our gate. 'The Form's gone,' I said.

'Gone?' said the lodger, looking at me with a good deal of respect. 'Do you mean actually posted?'

'I've just dropped it into the letter-box myself,' I said. 'I had a little help over filling it in.'

That same afternoon Lady B came to tea. She brought her knitting.

'How do you feel about the Invasion?' I said to her.

'Calm,' said Lady B. 'How do you?'

'Calm too,' I said, 'and nobody could be more surprised, because as a rule I am terrified of practically everything.'

'I think we are being Given Strength,' said Lady B. 'Like when people are going to have babies, and everybody goes about with white, drawn faces except the Expectant Mother, who is perfectly calm, because she *knows* everything is going to be all right. It is Nature's Way.'

'Great Britain as an expectant mother is quite a new one,' I said.

'And America is the Expectant Grandmother, worrying like mad because she is afraid it is all going to be too much for us,' said Lady B.

'And Mr Churchill is the Nurse, very calm and confident, and saying, "You'll be worse before you're better."'

I wonder the cartoonists haven't thought of it before now, don't you, Robert?

Always your affectionate Childhood's Friend,

HENRIETTA

My Dear Robert   March 12, 1941

I think the British Housewife is having a confusing as well as a difficult time just now. Not very long ago we were urged to fill up our store-cupboards with enough food to last us for a fortnight in case of Invasion. 'Up, Housewives, and at 'em!' was the slogan of the day, and, burning with patriotic zeal, we all rushed to the grocer's.

Filling up a store-cupboard is, of course, the greatest fun, and Matins and I spent a happy morning stowing away tins of tongues and soups and milk and fruit and a popular beef stew with veg in a very, very secret place, which I won't write down here in case this letter were to fall into Hitler's hands.

Charles raised his eyebrows rather at the weekly house-keeping cheque, until it was explained to him that it was all part of the Victory Campaign.

The glow of our pride and self-satisfaction had hardly had time to die down when I read in the paper one morning that a Power at Whitehall had made a speech in which he had said that he had been shocked—yes, *shocked*—to find that the British Public was Hoarding Food. The rest of his speech rather gave one the impression that he would take pleasure in personally and publicly horse-whipping anybody who had so much as a tin of pineapple chunks stowed away under the stairs.

Blushing hotly, Matins and I rushed to the secret hiding-place and unearthed our treasure. For the next fortnight Evensong and I fed Charles, who has a prejudice against eating tinned foods of any description, on mysterious and highly-seasoned dishes.

'Curry *again*, Henrietta?'

'Well, yes, Charles. It's warming this weather, don't you think?'

'What's this made of?'

'Oh, just bits, you know.'

'It looks a little like tongue to me,' said Charles, peering closely at his plate and dissecting a small piece in an unpleasant surgical manner.

'There might be one or two little bits of tongue in it, Charles.'

Next week was Invasion Week, and on opening my morning paper I read that the Housewife also could play her part by Staying Put, and doling out, with forethought and economy, those stores which she had wisely collected while the Germans were still on the other side of the Channel.

I gave a low groan and dropped the paper on the floor.

'What's the matter?' said Charles.

'I'm afraid the books will be rather high again this week, Charles.'

'Never mind,' said Charles kindly. 'They've been very low for the last fortnight.'

'I bet they have,' I said to myself, but I didn't say it

aloud, as I am a firm believer in letting sleeping dogs lie.

Isn't it funny the way the initials 'B.O.' always stand for something rather awful? In the chemists' advertisements before the war, of course, they stood for something so humiliating that it could only be alluded to by initials, and even then with shame. When Bill and the Linnet were small they used to mean 'Buzz Off'. Now they stand for Billeting Officer and Black-out, two of the biggest Bogeys of our lives.

The other day, when I was having my hair done, I composed a 1941 Folk Song called 'Black-outs Hey', which began—

> *Oh, come, my Love, come away, come away,*
> *And do the B.O. with Me-O.*

While I was under the drier i worked out a rather engaging little Folk Dance to go with it, in which the couples advanced, each holding two sticks with a piece of black cloth suspended between them, changed partners, set to corners, and, after a little Olde Worlde stamping and circling, advanced down the room in a long line, the black cloth held high above their heads like a long, dark ribbon.

I was so pleased with my idea that I took it to Mrs Whinebite, who is the Folk Dance and Song queen down here; but I am sorry to say she didn't think much of it.

'If you don't mind my saying so, Henrietta,' she said, 'I think it would look rather silly, and all that black stuff would quite spoil the brightness of the print frocks and sun-bonnets.'

'They might wear tin hats and gas-masks.'

'God forbid!' said Mrs Whinebite, closing her eyes.

'But Folk Dances are supposed to represent the spirit of the age, aren't they?' I said, for I was loth to abandon my idea without a struggle. 'In a few hundred years the gas-mask will probably have evolved into something quite quaint, such as a wreath of wild flowers worn round the nose and chin, and tied to the head with ribands gay.'

Something quite quaint

I thought it would please Mrs Whinebite to hear me say 'ribands' instead of 'ribbons', but by that time she wasn't even listening.

Always your affectionate Childhood's Friend,

HENRIETTA

April 9, 1941

My DEAR ROBERT

Charles held a stirrup-pump practice on the lawn after lunch on Sunday.

'Now, you, Henrietta, had better be on the hose, which is practically foolproof,' he said kindly. 'All you have to do is to crawl along with the dustbin lid in one hand and the hose-pipe in the other, taking care to keep your head not more than three inches from the ground, and with your gas-mask ready to be put on at a moment's notice.'

'It sounds too easy,' I said.

'As a matter of fact, it's perfectly simple,' said Charles. 'You use the spray on a bomb and the jet on burning wood-work. Just press this brass thing, and it changes from one to the other.'

'How do I know which is the spray and which is the jet?' I said.

'Try both,' said Charles patiently, 'and then you can see for yourself.'

'Oh, yes; of course.'

'The lodger had better pump,' said Charles, ' "for though she's little, yet she's fierce".'

'Like Hermia,' said the lodger.

'You've been educated,' said Charles admiringly.

'And what are you going to do, Charles?' I said.

'I shall probably be at the hospital, so it's no good counting on me,' said Charles. 'You women have got to stop the place burning down somehow. Now then, Henrietta, down you go.'

'It's very damp,' I said.

'Don't be a coward. Down you go.'

'What shall I do?' said Charles's mother, who is staying with us just now, and had come out to see what was happening.

Charles looked at her thoughtfully. 'You'd better run to and fro with refill buckets of water,' he said.

'O.K.,' said Grannie, and trotted off.

'Perhaps you'd better bring half a bucket at a time,' shouted Charles. 'After all, she is eighty-four,' he added to himself in an undertone.

Suddenly my spirits soared up like a rocket. How could Hitler ever dream for one single moment that there was the slightest chance of defeating people like us?

Last Wednesday I found Lady B in her greenhouse, repotting chrysanthemums. 'I am enjoying myself so much,' she said apologetically. 'Of course, one oughtn't to take one's attention off the onions for one single minute, but I couldn't bear to see these poor things suffering any more. Look at that!' she said triumphantly, as she heaved one out of its pot and held it up for me to see.

It was indeed a sorry sight. The roots had pressed on a hopeless quest for freedom all round the sides, and had even grown, in a pathetic cascade, out of a hole at the bottom of the flower-pot.

'That's just exactly how I feel,' I said, deeply moved by the spectacle.

Lady B looked at me for a moment, and then began putting fine mould into the large and spacious pot which was to be the chrysanthemum's new home.

*I found Lady B
in her greenhouse*

'It *is* awful, never getting away,' she said. 'But, after all, it's better to be bodily pot-bound than mentally pot-bound, like the Germans. Mentally *and* spiritually pot-bound,' she said, enjoying the expression, and we went in to tea strangely comforted.

Always your affectionate Childhood's Friend,

HENRIETTA

April 23, 1941

M Y DEAR ROBERT
Ever since last October I have been trying to make Charles buy a new overcoat. Every time I suggested a visit to our Cathedral Town Charles said he couldn't spare the time, and what was the matter with his old one, anyway? It

had cost enough, goodness knew, and he'd only had it six years.

I said it was a nice coat, but rather shiny. Charles said he liked it shiny, and there the matter rested for a time. But last week, when Faith ran into Charles just as he was stepping into his car, and stopped and got out her lipstick and pretended to use him as a looking-glass, it began to dawn, even on him, that perhaps it really was time he got a new one.

Last Saturday morning he suddenly appeared and said he'd just got time to rush in and buy himself a coat before lunch. I was quite stunned by this news and could only stand and stare.

'Hurry up, Henrietta,' said Charles. 'You know the shops shut at one.'

I dashed off to put away the mop which I happened to be holding in my hand and fell downstairs. I landed on my head, there was a loud cracking noise in my neck, and I thought what a silly way it was to get killed in the middle of a war. My hand seemed to be hurting a good deal, too. A Pott's fracture, no doubt, I thought grandly, remembering my V.A.D. days—or was it a Collis?

I lay on the floor with my eyes shut, feeling pleased that for some time I would be unable to dig in the garden,

. . . and fell downstairs

wash up, clean the bath, or take Perry for walks. I pictured myself propped up in bed, one arm in a sling, my head becomingly bandaged, and Charles tip-toeing in with a bunch of violets. My whole being, as they say, was flooded with happiness at the thought, and I groaned slightly.

Nothing happened, so I groaned again, and Matins poked her head over the banisters and said she *thought* she'd heard somebody falling downstairs, and Charles came out of the dining-room.

'What *have* you been doing, Henrietta?' he said crossly, and helped me to my feet.

'I think I've got a Pott's fracture, Charles,' I said.

'No, you haven't,' said Charles.

'My head, my head!' I wailed, feeling that things were not going according to plan.

'Is it bleeding?' said Charles.

'No.'

'Poor old girl,' he said, patting my shoulder kindly. 'Now, hurry up or the whole damn place will be shut up.'

I always enjoy going to Charles's tailors. The place has a pleasing ecclesiastical air, and all the shopmen, who are slightly deaf, look like bishops. We push open the door quietly, Charles takes off his hat, and we creep up the aisle.

'Yes, Sir?'

'I want a new overcoat.'

'Did you say socks, Sir?'

'No. Overcoat.'

We make a hushed entrance into the tailoring department, which is full of sober tweeds. On a stand, in a prominent position, is a pink evening tail-coat adorned with the Hunt's excruciating facings, a relic of the days of peace and plenty and a gesture of defiance to Hitler. One of the Dignitaries comes forward, his hands clasped, and a tape-measure hanging round his neck like a stole.

'I want a ready-made overcoat,' says Charles loudly and clearly. 'I haven't got time to come in and be fitted.' This remark is received in shocked silence.

'Your father used to say he'd sooner have no coat at all than a ready-made one, Sir,' says the Dignitary with the stole, looking down his nose.

'My father didn't have to work as hard as I do,' says Charles grimly, and we are led from the tailoring into a very small lift, where we find ourselves pressed against the Dignitary's watch-chain.

The ready-to-wear department is deserted and there is a large spider's web on the overcoat stand. Nevertheless, Charles buys himself an extremely nice, warm, pre-war coat with a touch of blue in the tweed.

My finger is still very purple and swollen, and I show it to everybody with pride. Unfortunately, I am able to weed and wash up, but I have had to draw your pictures with my left hand this week, Robert.

Always your affectionate Childhood's Friend,

HENRIETTA

April 30, 1941

M Y DEAR ROBERT
On the radio there is talk of invasion but let's not think about that. I am going to tell you instead about Mrs Savernack and Perry.

It was yesterday. Mrs Savernack came round looking very worked up but ten years younger than usual. She pressed a damp, cold parcel into my hand and appeared almost too moved to speak.

'What is it?' I said.

Mrs Savernack gulped. 'Meat for Perry,' she said in a strangled voice.

I threw my arms round her neck and we mingled our tears. Then a dreadful thought struck me. She has had some sheep billeted on her in one of her fields for the last fortnight, and more than once Charles has remarked that whenever he goes to the house to see Mr Savernack, who has influenza, Mrs Savernack, rendered desperate by the

We mingled our tears

sufferings of her dogs, is to be seen standing at the window, staring out hungrily and fingering her gun.

I drew away from her and looked searchingly into her face, where the tears were not yet dry. 'Where did you get it?' I said.

'It's all right, Henrietta,' she said. 'It's horse.'

'Not Gertrude?' I said, in a hushed whisper.

'No, not *my* horse—just horse. The dogs like it all right, but it makes 'em smell a bit.'

I couldn't wait for Charles to come home to lunch, so I rang him up at his surgery. 'I've got wonderful news for you,' I said.

'Is the war over?' said Charles hopefully.

'No. But I've got some meat for Perry.'

'You haven't!'

'I have! It's horse. Mrs Savernack says it makes them smell a bit.'

'Well, Perry never has been what you might call an Attar of Roses.'

'No. I don't suppose we shall notice much difference.'

'Horrid little dog!' said Charles with deep affection, and rang off.

My dear Robert, the radio is still talking of invasions, but outside the seagulls are beginning to get ready for the Summer Visitors. No bathing-hut attendant or lodging-house keeper looks forward with as much pleasure to a good season as do the seagulls. About this time of the year they begin preening and prinking in a very self-conscious manner, standing on one leg on the chimney-pots on cold days, and standing, still on one leg, on the windlasses on warm days and gazing out to sea with noble expressions on their faces. This behaviour, which is intended as a sort of curtain-raiser, provokes many exclamations of admiration from the Spring Visitors, who are too cold to sit about and give the birds their full attention. We call the visitors Grockles. Don't ask me why. In Cornwall they're Emmets. Mrs Savernack would know. She—God bless her—knows everything.

Always your affectionate Childhood's Friend,

HENRIETTA

My Dear Robert   May 7, 1941

It really is extraordinary how one can become accustomed to anything in time. I shall always remember the first time the siren went off, and how we all jumped out of bed and went down to the scullery, and my knees shook. Now, when it wails on and off all night, we just turn over in bed and grunt. But the other night was different.

'Do you hear a funny noise?' I said to Charles.

'Yes,' said Charles.

'What is it?'

'Oh, somebody firing something at somebody,' said Charles, and fell asleep again.

I got up and looked out of the window, and saw what looked like every house in the place ablaze. The next minute there was a deafening crash on the landing, which I thought must surely be an incendiary bomb until I remembered that the pre-arranged signal of danger with our lodger in the attics was to be a saucepan thrown down the well of the stairs. A second later she appeared in the doorway, a pocket Amazon, holding aloft the dustbin-lid which she takes up to bed with her every night.

'Come on!'
shouted the lodger

'Come on!' shouted the lodger. 'Now's our chance! Incendiaries.'

'What a racket you two are making!' said Charles peevishly.

'But Charles! The place is on fire!'

'Do you mean this house is on fire?' said Charles, showing interest for the first time.

'Not actually this house.'

'Well, I can't leave the telephone, in case I'm wanted at the hospital,' said Charles, and composed himself to slumber once more.

The lodger and I went into the garden, and the sight which met our eyes was better than any firework display, but it was all at the other end of the town, and everywhere the lights were going out one by one as though snuffed by giant fingers.

'Everybody's putting them out except us,' wailed the lodger, beating on her dustbin-lid in a distraught manner.

Then we saw the incendiary bomb blazing merrily in the Simpkins's garden. We knew Colonel Simpkins would be out with the A.R.P., and Mrs Simpkins was alone in the house. I rushed back to the porch for a sand-bag, found it was too heavy to lift, made a supreme effort, struggled with it for a few yards, and fell down.

In the end we had to put it on the dustbin-lid and carry it between us.

'I hope it isn't one of those explosive ones,' I said nervously, as we reeled, panting, up the garden path, and the lodger gave a contemptuous snort. The next minute a little figure staggered out from behind some bushes. It was Mrs Simpkins, wearing corduroy trousers, which she had treasured for goodness knows how many months against such an emergency, over her nightgown.

'It's my bomb!' cried Mrs Simpkins, like a lion defending its cubs.

'We've come to put it out for you,' said the lodger.

'I don't want you to put it out for me. I want to put it out for myself.'

'The sand-bag is too heavy for you.'

'It isn't. It isn't. I've been practising.'

'Ours has got more sand in it.'

'It's my bomb!'

We glared at each other, our faces distorted with passion in the lurid light. Suddenly the bomb went out. It must have been burning for some time, and perhaps it wasn't a very good one, anyway.

Always your affectionate Childhood's Friend,

HENRIETTA

May 14, 1941

M Y DEAR ROBERT
There are rumours that we are to have another change of soldiery, and that means another row of fortifications. Sometimes the new soldiery pulls down the fortifications it finds when it arrives, and sometimes it just adds to them, but it always gives us to understand that until it came we had been but poorly protected, but that now we may sleep peacefully in our beds, secure from Invasion.

We already have many guns which poke out of unexpected places. Some of them don't even poke, and are so cleverly concealed that even visiting generals are deceived.

The gun I hate most is the one which is hidden behind a little trap-door. Every morning when I take Perry for his walk on what nature and the British Army have left us of the cliff path, the little trap-door is open and a wicked-looking muzzle peers out with a baleful, one-eyed expression. It always seems to be pointing straight at me. If I hug the wall it still points at me, and when I move over to the other side and risk my life by walking on the extreme edge of the cliff the gun slews slowly round in my direction.

I remind myself that I am the daughter and grand-daughter of soldiers, and try not to walk more quickly. I remember Mr Churchill's speech and the Charge of the Light Brigade. I move to the middle of the path, and so does the gun, and I remember how our father never allowed us to point guns at anybody, not even toy ones, because it was a Dangerous Thing To Do. I remember that yesterday was real gun practice day, with the cliff path closed to the public, and I wonder whether just one teeny little shell may not have been left in by mistake. I remember the Linnet's remark that you simply wouldn't believe what a lot of soldiers are in hospital because guns have gone off when people didn't know they were loaded.

Mrs Whinebite gave a party during War Weapons

Week. We each had to bring half a crown and our own tea, and though we were all glad to do what we could for the W.W.W., everybody felt she had no right to take all the credit herself, though the anachronism idea was hers. In the corner of each invitation was written, 'Please bring a War Anachronism with you.' This created a good deal of excitement in the place, and for three days the Whinebites' telephone never stopped ringing, because some people didn't know what an anachronism was, and the others rang up to make sure they had got the idea all right.

The Whinebites' telephone never stopped ringing

The party was quite a success. It started rather stickily because it was a very cold day and Mrs Whinebite is the sort of person who never lights a fire once the spring cleaning is done. But the Conductor threw a lighted match into the grate and pretended he had done it by mistake, and soon we had a good blaze and everybody cheered up. We made rather a lot of crumbs, eating out of our paper bags; but, as Faith said, that was Mrs Whinebite's fault for not providing us with plates.

Some of the anachronisms were quite good. Of course, a lot of people brought what had once been boxes of chocolates, and there were a few pathetic dance programmes, and one or two city-banquet menus which people kept reading aloud to each other. Faith brought a Mrs Beeton cookery book which began, 'Take the yolks of eight eggs and a pint of cream.' The Admiral brought an A.A. route for a motoring tour from here to the north of Scotland, and Mrs Simpkins's brother, old General Tayling, who is eighty-four, came as himself. He said he was an anachronism of this war if ever there was one. We voted for the prize, which was an extremely handsome one —three large onions. Lady B won it with her quotation, 'The Carpenter said nothing but "The butter's spread too thick."'

Always your affectionate Childhood's Friend,

HENRIETTA

May 21, 1941

MY DEAR ROBERT
Everybody is beginning to think that it is time Faith gave the Conductor a definite answer one way or the other. He has been losing a lot of weight during the last few months, and though that may be due rather to the rationing than to Faith, his behaviour to the choir, ever since Christmas, can only be the result of nerves strained to breaking-point.

Last Tuesday when we sang an F sharp instead of an F natural three times in succession, which is really nothing for this choir, the Conductor threw down his bâton and walked out.

I was very angry with Faith for causing so much unnecessary suffering, and when she came round yesterday afternoon while I was weeding the kitchen-garden path, I determined to take her to task, as they say.

'How nice you look, Faith,' I said, which was a bad beginning, but I just couldn't help saying it.

'This old rag?' said Faith, as she always does. Then

she lay down among the bluebells under the mulberry-tree and said she'd been up with the A.R.P. all night and was worn out. The bluebells exactly matched her eyes, but I hardened my heart against her, and said,

'You don't do a rap of work during the day, anyhow.'

Faith sat up. 'Why are you being so unkind to me, Henrietta?' she said piteously.

'Why are *you* being so unkind, if it comes to that?' I said, stabbing at a large dandelion with my hoe.

'I can't marry him,' said Faith sadly. 'He snores.' And she lay down among the bluebells.

I put down my hoe. 'Faith,' I said, 'how do you know he snores?'

'I hear him at the A.R.P.,' said Faith, with her eyes shut.

In silence I picked up my hoe and renewed my attack upon the dandelion. After a little time Faith sat up again. 'Henrietta,' she said, opening her bluebell eyes very wide, 'why did you say that?'

'Let it pass,' I said. 'I always thought you sat up on hard chairs all night with your gas-masks on. This is the first I've heard of beds and snoring.'

'There's only one bed,' said Faith.

'Surely you don't *all*—'

'No, no. Of course not. It's a very small camp affair. The one who's on duty all night, whether there's an alert or not, has The Bed.'

I laid down my hoe a second time and joined her among the bluebells, for I found this conversation of absorbing interest.

'Tell me, Faith,' I said, 'do the men get into pyjamas?'

'No,' said Faith. 'They take off their collars and ties.'

'Naturally.'

'All except Mr Savernack, who keeps his on and lies *outside* the blanket.'

Outside the blanket

'Quite likely it is Mrs Savernack's wish, Faith.'

'Quite likely, Henrietta.'

There was a silence while I reflected, not for the first time, that the Civil Defence has all the excitement of this war.

'Colonel Simpkins is a very quiet sleeper,' said Faith.

'I have always looked upon him as the perfect type of English gentleman.'

'At eleven o'clock the Admiral comes and puts out the light and says "No more talking".'

'That must be rather dull.'

'Yes. But you see, it isn't fair to the one in The Bed if we chatter all night.'

'Quite.'

Soon afterwards Faith went away. I walked to the gate with her, for she seemed rather sad. 'I shouldn't bother too much about the snoring,' I said, squeezing her arm. 'A lot of people snore in camp-beds who never snore anywhere else.'

'Do you think so?' said Faith, brightening a little.

'I'm sure of it. And I think it's Simply Wonderful What You Are Doing, Faith.' I think it is the duty of all those without brassards to make this remark as often as

136

possible. It never fails to gratify, and in this case it worked wonders. Faith positively danced down the road, and stopped at the corner to wave.

Soon after she had gone the Conductor appeared. When I told him Faith had gone he said he wouldn't wait, and for the second time that afternoon I left my weeding to walk to the gate.

'Faith's been telling me about the A.R.P.,' I said. 'I had no idea people had to sleep down there all night. I think it's Simply Wonderful—'

But the Conductor wasn't listening. A tender smile lit up his face. 'She does snore so, bless her heart!' he said. 'You know, Henrietta, you simply wouldn't believe such a loud noise could be made by such a darling little nose.'

Always your affectionate Childhood's Friend,

HENRIETTA

June 4, 1941

M Y DEAR ROBERT
Lady B is going to sell her house. Everybody was very much upset when they heard the news, for she has always seemed to us to be in her perfect setting, and her evacuees set up a doleful howling. However, she told them that if there was room in her new flat she would take the one who was the least trouble with her. She says after that their behaviour was so exemplary it quite embarrassed her.

For a long time she has been saying that she couldn't afford the house, but it was when the old gardener had to give up work, and there wasn't another to be had, that she decided that it was time to go.

'I'm too old to dig,' she said, 'and it isn't fair to neglect a garden these days.'

It was just like Lady B to be so plucky and sensible about it, and when I went up to tea one day last week it was a shock to find her sitting on the floor with a child's doll on her lap and the tears rolling down her cheeks.

With a child's doll on her lap

'It was Sarah's,' she said in a choked voice while she fumbled about for a handkerchief.

I passed her mine in silence. Sarah was Lady B's very precious daughter who died as a V.A.D. in the last war.

'She was a rather plain little girl,' said Lady B, dabbing at her eyes. 'Freckly, you know, and with cut knees, but such a darling. This is the doll she loved best. Her name is Hermione.'

Hermione's eyes opened with a click and she said 'Ma-ma.'

'Keep her,' I said.

'Good gracious, no!' said Lady B briskly, and she got up off the floor and put Hermione back into her cradle. 'I'm going to get rid of everything which isn't really necessary. I shall keep one fork and one spoon and one knife and one chair and one bed, and my life will be simple and idyllic.'

'And what about a table?'

'A table, of course.'

'And what about the evacuee?'

'Don't be tiresome, Henrietta.'

'It will be nice not to have to bother about weeds,' I said wistfully.

'It will be heavenly!' said Lady B with fervour. 'I shall have a window-box in which I shall dig with my one fork.'

'I think I shall stop being sorry for you,' I said.

'I should think so, indeed!' said Lady B, pouring out the tea. 'It is the best thing that has happened to me for ages, and you mustn't take any notice if I get a bit weepy and sentimental; it is the privilege of age.'

She was quite her old self again.

'I'm not at all sure that I shan't grow mustard and cress in my window-box.'

'And you could cut it with your one pair of nail-scissors.'

Lady B smiled happily. 'The secret of happiness is to adopt *this* attitude towards possessions,' she said—and she made a pushing-away gesture with her hands—'rather than this,' and she pulled an imaginary treasure to her bosom. 'Once you can drop the grabbing habit everything is plain sailing. I'm all right, because my family has been coming down in the world for so many generations that it's sort of in my blood. It's the ones on the up-grade who are finding it so difficult to get into reverse. Poor things,' she added, with deep sympathy.

'You are a philosopher,' I said, 'and young men ought to sit at your feet.'

'I can't imagine anything nicer,' said Lady B.

Always your affectionate Childhood's Friend,

HENRIETTA

MY DEAR ROBERT   June 18, 1941
      The Conductor gave two concerts last week, one here, and one in an outlying village. He has been in bed ever since. Here we had our usual rather sullen audience composed of people who had been bludgeoned into buying tickets and who would rather have been playing bridge. The most exciting moment of the afternoon, as far as I was concerned, was when I came in with a loud fluting note a whole bar too soon, but with great presence of mind I turned and gave Faith, who was standing next to me, a Look, and the Conductor, thinking she was the culprit, smiled indulgently.

I turned and gave Faith a Look

      The concert in the outlying village was much more fun because the Women's Institute hall was packed with people who all wanted to be there, and were determined to enjoy themselves at all costs. The front seats, which had gone up sixpence this year and were now two shillings, were gratifyingly full of London Visitors, and officers who are billeted in the village. They had come partly because their landladies had sold them tickets, partly because they felt it was the duty of the gentry to uphold Village Effort, but mostly because they hoped it would be like the gramophone record of 'Our Village Concert', and that they'd get a good laugh. The back seats came partly to laugh at their friends on the stage, and partly to laugh at the gentry laughing at the village . . .

Faith was looking divine, as usual. But how long can it last? We were all dreadfully sorry for her the other day when clothes rationing was announced. She came up to our house straight after the broadcast looking white and drawn.

'I've given up offering people my whisky, Faith,' said Charles gently as he led her to the sofa, 'but I'd like you to have some now.'

'I'd sooner have some sherry,' said Faith in a choked voice.

Charles filled a port glass to the brim and handed it to her. 'You can still buy hats,' he said tenderly.

'Hats!' said Faith. 'Nobody wears a hat in the country!' and she tossed off her sherry as though it were vodka.

'And you've got an awful lot of clothes to go on with,' I said, and Faith gave me a withering look.

'It wouldn't matter so much if the make-up wasn't going off the market,' she said gloomily. 'You can get away with no clothes if you've got plenty of make-up.'

'I'm sure you can,' said Charles admiringly as he refilled her glass.

'My grandmother used to tell me that once when she particularly wanted to cut a dash at a dance she made herself some rouge out of red geranium petals and was the Belle of the Ball. In fact, that was the night she hooked grandfather.'

'I suppose she mixed the petals with something?' said Faith, with deep interest. Then the Conductor came in and Faith, who was starting on her third glass of sherry and cheering up, waved to him and said she had decided to have an evening coat made of patchwork silk.

'Motley's the only wear,' said the Conductor. Then he sat down beside her on the sofa and took her hand. 'I just want you to know,' he said, 'that you can have *all* my coupons.'

'Are they transferable?' said Faith, who was greatly touched by this sign of devotion.

'Only among families,' said Charles.

'Well—' said the Conductor, with a meaning look.

Charles saw them to the gate. When he came back he said that if the Conductor didn't pull it off this time he never would.

The next morning I met Lady B. 'My dear,' she said, 'Faith has gone stark staring mad.'

'Has she accepted him?' I asked eagerly.

'Not as far as I know,' said Lady B. 'But she's got her garden cramjam full of the most awful red geraniums.'

Always your affectionate Childhood's Friend,

HENRIETTA

July 2, 1941

MY DEAR ROBERT
One of the prize gardens in these parts was thrown open to the public one day last week. Charles and I both went, Charles because the sixpence a head entrance fee was in aid of the Cottage Hospital, and I because I wanted to see the garden.

I think it is the loveliest garden I know. To begin with, it is large, but not so large as to make the owner's house look like a tool shed. Then it has a little stream running along the bottom edge, as all good gardens

should have; but best of all,
everything in it seems to be
growing there because it is
the right and proper place for
it to grow, and not because
some determined person
with a spade has made a hole
and shoved it in.

Charles and I wandered
round in a depressed way,
wondering how we could ever
have dared to call the jungle
which surrounds our house
a garden. Here there were no
weeds, no slugs, snails, or
greenfly, and everything

*One of the prize gardens was
thrown open to the public*

seemed to be growing healthily and happily in the right
shape. Most of the plants were so rare that they had little
metal notice boards with long Latin names on them stuck
into the ground beside them, and the few we did recognize
were new and surprising colours.

'That's a delphinium, Charles.'

'Don't be silly, Henrietta, it's pink.'

'All the same, it *is* a delphinium, Charles.'

Charles sighed. 'Let's go and have a look at the veg,'
he said.

But if he hoped to see signs of neglect in the vegetable
garden he was doomed to disappointment.

We returned to the flower garden in silence. The
owner was walking about with a shooting-stick, a proud
and happy man, talking to his guests, advising, explaining,
and listening patiently to long, boring stories of other
people's garden troubles.

'I think those azaleas are *the* most beautiful things

I've ever seen,' said a guest in a hushed gardening voice.

'Yes, but look at this little beast,' said the owner, poking fretfully at a rather less exuberant specimen with his shooting-stick. 'It came from Mongolia and I *can't* get it to settle down.'

'You see, Charles,' I said wistfully, 'he isn't even conceited.'

Suddenly Charles clutched my arm and pointed with a shaking finger. 'Look!' he said. 'Look, Henrietta!'

There it was, growing low on the ground, urban, squat, and packed with guile, like the Cambridge people in Rupert Brooke's poem, and with roots, as well we knew, in Australia.

'Bindweed!' we shouted, and leaped forward like hounds at a kill.

The owner came hurrying across what I must call the sward, because grass seems too ordinary a word. 'I see you are admiring those dwarf lupins,' he said. 'People often cry out when they see them.'

'I really must congratulate you on your lovely garden,' said Charles, who was now in the highest spirits.

'Are you a gardener, Mrs Brown?' said the owner.

'I am a weeder,' I said.

His wife, who had joined the party, leant towards me and said in a low voice, 'What is your favourite weed?'

'Groundsel,' I said, without a moment's hesitation.

'Groundsel is my favourite, too,' said the owner's wife. 'It comes out of the ground very sweetly, doesn't it?' and we gave each other a long Look, fraught, as they say, with understanding.

The owner walked with us to the gate, and we thanked him for his garden, and told him he ought to be a very happy man, because he worked hard all day at the thing he liked doing best in the world, and was making a bit of England more and more beautiful when such a lot of it was being made more and more ugly.

'I like to think of it in that way,' said the owner.

Always your affectionate Childhood's Friend,

HENRIETTA

July 30, 1941

MY DEAR ROBERT

I wonder if you remember my telling you how Hilary and Pops swept me into their Blood Room in our Cathedral City Hospital and drew a reluctant drop from my ear?

I have had to pay dearly for this girlish prank, let me tell you, and you can imagine my horror when I got a postcard telling me I was urgently needed to give a blood transfusion at the Cottage Hospital on the following Tuesday.

Charles was very cross when I told him about it. 'You shouldn't let yourself in for this sort of thing, Henrietta,' he said. 'You know perfectly well that it's Evensong's night out. Supposing you want to lie down or something when you get home? Who's going to get the dinner?'

I said I would ask Evensong to change her day, and did people ever die giving their blood?

At this Charles and the Linnet, who was home for the day, went into shrieks of laughter and said, 'Not very often.'

Tuesday found me in a considerable state of nerves. 'Don't worry,' said Charles kindly. 'Any weakness or discomfort you may feel will be purely psychological, and you may get a glass of beer when it is all over.'

At 3 p.m. I dressed myself carefully in the quiet clothes suitable to a donor, and crept up to the hospital. The first thing I saw as I walked in at the door was Mrs Savernack lying on a sort of stretcher and apparently dying. As I bent over her and took her hand, I suddenly realized how fond I was of her, and regretted all the unkind things I had said about her in the past.

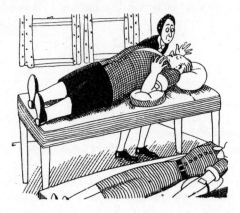

Lying on a sort of stretcher

Mrs Savernack opened her eyes and said, 'Where's that cup of tea?'

'Here you are,' said an exquisite V.A.D., appearing round the corner.

'There's a lot to be said for the old custom of blood-letting,' said Mrs Savernack heartily, smacking her lips as she handed back the empty cup. 'Hullo, Henrietta! What are you goggling at? You don't mean to say you're going to try and give some blood?'

'I shall try, and no doubt I shall succeed,' I said with dignity, for Mrs Savernack's continual assumption that I am unable to perform any useful duty is annoying, and I stopped regretting all the unkind things I had said about her in the past. As I was led away, I heard her say in a loud whisper, 'You'll have trouble with that woman.'

Determined, after this, to give my very life blood without a murmur, I lay down on a stretcher, bared my arm, and turned away my head. A young R.A.M.C. lieutenant appeared and various things were done which I tried not to think about. 'Keep on clenching and unclenching your hand,' he said kindly. 'It prevents that unpleasant bubbling sensation.'

I clenched and unclenched my hand as hard as I could, for I found the bubbling sensation very unpleasant indeed, and the R.A.M.C. lieutenant said, 'That's right —you're getting along nicely.' He had golden hair and was so like you, Robert, at the age of twenty-five, that I could hardly take my eyes off him.

I lay on my stretcher and decided that this blood transfusion business was child's play. It wasn't hurting, the bubbling sensation had stopped, the sun shone on the lieutenant's hair, and my V.A.D. sat beside me, a model of efficiency and comfort. Various people lay about on stretchers, looking yellow but quite calm; and, contrary to my expectations, blood was not being splashed all over the walls. Indeed, if you averted your eyes from sinister red bottles rotating in a sort of dignified dance on gramophones beside each bed, you might think the whole thing was nothing more than a cosy, communal siesta.

'All right?' said the R.A.M.C. lieutenant. How bored he was with blood! I felt so sorry for him.

I turned my head and took a look at my V.A.D. sitting beside me so neat, sweet and calm, and I glowed with pride in the Old Regiment. 'I was a V.A.D. in the last war,' I said, 'but I never did anything exciting like this.'

'Exciting?' said the V.A.D. with a sigh.

I wanted to tell her how splendid I thought she and the other V.A.D.s were when suddenly a sweat broke out on me. I could feel it trickling down inside my shirt. 'Psychological be blowed, Charles!' I said to myself. 'I'm dying.'

'All over,' said the V.A.D. brightly, and she bent my arm up. 'Like a cup of tea?'

'No,' I said.

This seemed to shake her, and she took one of my pillows away, loosened the belt of my cardigan, and held smelling-salts under my nose.

'I think you'd better put some of that blood back,' I said weakly.

'Keep perfectly still,' said the lieutenant, who had, presumably, witnessed so many blood-transfusion deaths that he wasn't going to start getting excited over mine.

But I didn't die. After a time I sat up and had some delicious tea out of a thick white mug. Mrs Savernack poked her head round the door. 'Have any trouble with her?' she asked hopefully.

I looked imploringly at my V.A.D. and the lieutenant. They looked at me, and then they looked at each other. 'None at all,' they said together and very firmly.

I hope they both get George Crosses.

Always your affectionate Childhood's Friend,

HENRIETTA

August 27, 1941

MY DEAR ROBERT
Lady B is very indignant about a picture she saw in the paper of Russian women with baskets in one hand and rifles in the other. 'Why don't they give us rifles? If every woman in Britain had a rifle,' said Lady B, her eyes glittering wildly, 'just think what they could do.'

'I'd rather not!' said Charles, shuddering.

But I began thinking what a help a rifle would be during morning shopping.

LADY SHOPPER: Any cornflakes, Mr Green?

148

MR GREEN: No cornflakes, Madam.

LADY SHOPPER: No cornflakes *at all*, Mr Green?

MR GREEN: None, Madam.

LADY SHOPPER (leaning across the counter and fingering the trigger of her rifle): *Are you quite sure there are no cornflakes,* Mr Green?

MR GREEN: Well, Madam, perhaps just one.

(He dives under the counter and produces the last packet, which he has been keeping for his wife's cousin.)

And just think how the Woman Who Took Somebody Else's Turn in the fish shop would fall, riddled with bullets, just as she was handed her cod steak—and serve her right, too. The more I thought about it the more I agreed with Lady B that it would be a good thing to arm the women of Britain.

But Faith thought it would be a mistake. She said there were so many rows in the place just now that it would lead to endless blood-feuds and vendettas, and practically nobody would be left alive at the end of the week. She looked at us very meaningly as she said this, and Lady B and I got rather red and shuffled with our feet, because, I must tell you, Robert, that Faith and Lady B and Mrs Savernack and I have been involved in one of the most stupendous rows which has ever taken place. Now it is all over, it is Lady B and I, the two more or less innocent parties, who shuffle, and Mrs Savernack and Faith who do not.

It came about like this. I happened to meet Mrs Savernack in the street one morning and she told me that Gladys, their cook, who has been with them for ten years, had given notice, and that Mr Savernack was so upset he'd had to go to Charles for something to make him sleep.

I said how sorry I was, and passed on, and that was the beginning of the row, though it looks harmless enough so far, doesn't it?

Next day was Sunday, and Faith arrived at Lady B's after church, and immediately began a moan because her cook wanted to be a W.A.A.F.

I said, casually, that Mrs Savernack's Gladys was leaving, and poor Mr Savernack couldn't sleep. Faith hurried away soon afterwards with a determined look on her face, and I remember saying to Lady B that I hoped she'd set about acquiring Gladys in a tactful manner. A cloud a good deal smaller than a man's hand; but still, a cloud.

Faith set about acquiring Gladys in the most tactless way possible. She went to the Savernacks' house that evening through the tradesmen's entrance, and tapped on the kitchen window. Gladys, who is an extremely nervous woman at the best of times, and who has lived in dread of escaped Dartmoor convicts ever since she came to Devon, set up a shrill screaming. In rushed Mrs Savernack, to find Gladys with her apron over her head and Faith half-way through the kitchen window saying, 'Double your wages and a portable wireless.'

'What is this?' thundered Mrs Savernack.

'Oh,' said Faith, who ought to have been confused, but wasn't, 'Henrietta said something about

'Double your wages and a portable wireless'

Mr Savernack's headaches because Gladys was leaving.'

'Who?'

'Henrietta,' said Faith, who could so easily have said she'd heard a rumour about Gladys at the Bee. Mrs Savernack seized her by the arm and rushed her, as the Red Queen rushed Alice, down the road to our house.

Charles was out, and Lady B and I were spending a quiet evening together—at least, that had been the idea. We were enjoying a cosy chat on carnation cuttings, when the door burst open and Mrs Savernack rushed in, dragging Faith behind her.

'How dare you betray the sacred trust placed in you as a Doctor's Wife?' she said in a voice choked with rage.

'What have I done, Mrs Savernack?' I cried, starting to my feet, for my wifely conscience is never clear.

'You told Faith that Gladys was leaving.'

'I don't see what that has to do with Charles,' said Lady B.

'I suppose you'll say Henry's headaches are nothing to do with Charles?' said Mrs Savernack, rounding on her.

'Of course, if I'd known Henrietta was betraying a trust—' said Faith, throwing me to the lions.

'Henrietta is always most discreet,' said Lady B.

'She'd have a better chance if you didn't spoil her so,' said Mrs Savernack.

By this time we were all so angry there was no drawing back. Faith and Mrs Savernack, who in some strange way had become allies, told Lady B and me exactly what they thought of us, and we did the same. I always stammer when I'm angry, and a lot of my best bits were lost, but Lady B got in some good ones. I don't remember all that was said, and perhaps it is just as well, but I distinctly remember Lady B telling Mrs Savernack she was fat, insensitive and noisy, and somebody told me I was conceited and artificial, and my vagueness was a pose.

At the end of five minutes we were all white with rage and mortification, and nobody heard the telephone. Then Charles came in to say Mr Savernack had rung up to say that Gladys felt she couldn't leave the dogs, and had decided to stay after all.

Mrs Savernack and Faith went off quite jauntily, arm in arm, but Lady B and I had to be given whisky to stop our legs shaking. Charles laughed a lot when we told him about the row. He said it was better than saying things behind each other's backs, anyway.

Always your affectionate Childhood's Friend,

HENRIETTA

September 10, 1941

My DEAR ROBERT

When I was shopping in the street the other day, I suddenly caught sight of myself in a glass, and, my word, Robert, it gave me a shock—two strained and popping eyes crowned by a worried frown, nose slightly unpowdered, deep lines, as the beauty specialist would say, running from nose to chin, and lips so tightly compressed that it was impossible to say whether they had been decently coloured that morning or not.

'Good heavens!' I cried aloud. 'This is terrible!'

'What is?' said Mrs Savernack, who was just coming out of the butcher's.

'My face,' I said.

'Is it?' said Mrs Savernack, without looking at me, and added passionately: 'I do think Thompson is *unfair* with his suet.'

I walked slowly up the street, and noticed that every

woman with a shopping basket had the Shopping Face. The contrast between them and the visitors, who were living in hotels or had landladies to do the shopping for them, and had only come out to buy picture postcards, was almost frightening. Then I saw Lady B sailing down the street like a stately galleon. Her face was calm and placid as well as being nicely made-up. In her hand she carried an enormous basket which was full to overflowing.

I dashed across the road and seized her by the hand. 'Darling Lady B!' I said. 'How do you do it?'

'Do what, Henrietta?'

'Look so calm and lovely in the middle of this battlefield.'

'I don't always *feel* calm,' said Lady B. 'But when I begin to want to scream I do this.' She took me by the arm and led me through the little alley-way which runs beside the ironmonger's to the sea. 'I stand here,' said Lady B, 'and look at the sea, and then I take six deep breaths and say, "Thank goodness there's enough of something." Then I go back and finish my shopping.'

'Thank goodness there's enough of something'

The sea was looking very lovely that morning—a deep indigo on the horizon, fading to grey—and there was obviously a great deal of it. Fortified, I returned to the grocer's and waited my turn in the queue.

After I had given my order, Mr Green leant across the counter and whispered, 'I've got a quarter of sultanas here if you'd care for them.'

'Mr Green!' I said, and sat down suddenly on a chair, for my legs had given way beneath me.

By the time I got home I felt so exhilarated by the thought of Home-Made Cake for Bill and Linnet's next visit that I decided to put the energy to some use and started on the windows.

The strips of material which I had pasted on so carefully a year ago were now covered in leprous spots and it was a relief to get rid of them. I was engaged upon this pleasing task when I saw Lady B coming up the garden path, and I dropped a little strip of wet linen on her.

'God bless my soul!' said Lady B. 'I suppose that was you, Henrietta. Can I come up?'

'Of course,' I said.

'I'm glad you're taking that stuff off,' said Lady B, arriving slightly out of breath in my bedroom. 'Are you going to paste net all over the glass?'

'No,' I said, 'I am not. This winter is going to be quite depressing enough without having to live in a perpetual twilight as well.'

'I couldn't agree with you more,' said Lady B, settling herself comfortably on my bed.

I lifted the corner of a linen strip with my finger-nail and pulled. It came away with a delicious tearing sound. 'Fascinating!' said Lady B.

'I always imagined myself doing this while the bells were pealing for victory,' I said.

'There's still the black-out to tear down,' said Lady B. 'That will be most enjoyable.'

'When I pasted these strips on,' I said as I polished the glass with a duster, 'I was in a blue funk. I couldn't settle to anything, I was so frightened. But in some peculiar way, pasting strips of old table-cloths all over the windows steadied me. I felt much better after I'd done it.'

'I believe all those pasting instructions by the B.B.C.

were nothing but a sedative to housewives,' said Lady B. 'There are times when I think our Government understands us better than we think it does.'

'It's funny how much less frightened one is now, because, of course, there's just as much reason to be frightened, if not more.'

'We are given Strength,' said Lady B serenely. 'But come along, Henrietta. Stuff those rags in the waste-paper basket. I expect the kettle's boiling.'

Always your affectionate Childhood's Friend,

HENRIETTA

November 5, 1941

MY DEAR ROBERT
Yesterday there was a loud rat-a-tat-tat at the front door, and I rushed downstairs thinking it was a telegram. It wasn't a telegram, but a large, heavy, exciting-looking parcel.

'Here you are,' said the postman, beaming like Father Christmas, 'one-and-a-penny to pay.'

'My goodness!' I said. 'How exciting! What do you think it is?'

'Something good, by the look of it,' said the postman.

I carried the parcel into the kitchen, and Evensong and I turned it over, shook it, smelt it, pressed it and examined the labels.

'Funny-looking stamps, aren't they?' said Evensong.

'They're Australian stamps. Look, that's a lyre-bird. Isn't it pretty?'

'How do you know it's a lyre-bird?' said Evensong, who doubts my intelligence.

'I used to live in Australia once.'

'Well, I never!' said Evensong, staring at me.

Inside the wrappings was a sealed tin. Evensong, who wields a pretty tin-opener, soon dealt with that. Inside the tin were packages.

'Sugar!' said Evensong, with a glad shout.

'Sultanas!'

'Marmalade!'

'Tea!'—'Tongue!'— 'Asparagus tips!'—'Cheese!'

'Butter-scotch!' 'Oh, Evensong! A little tin of honey!'

Evensong and I stared at each other in silence across the kitchen-table. 'I shall make plum duff for dinner tonight,' said Evensong, in a dreamy voice.

'Sultanas! Marmalade!'

After Evensong had extracted a generous portion of sultanas and sugar, we arranged the packages on a tray, which I carried about with me from room to room. When Faith rang up later I told her what had happened, and the news spread like wildfire. By seven o'clock quite a lot of people had been in to feast their eyes, and Evensong began to be nervous, and said she thought we ought to keep it all under lock and key.

'Anything happened?' said Charles, as he hung his hat up in the hall.

'Cornucopia has happened, Charles.'

'What do you mean?'

I held up the tray which I was carrying into the drawing-room for the evening. Charles, his eyes bulging out of his head, approached on tiptoe and touched each package with his finger, as though he doubted its reality. 'Where did they come from?' he whispered.

'Australia. Here's the card. It isn't anybody we know.'

Charles looked at me with a new respect. 'Somebody must have read one of your mouldy little stories,' he said in an astonished voice.

We had plum duff for dinner, real plum duff, as only an unhampered Evensong can make it, thick with sultanas, and sweet. Afterwards Charles called for the last half-decanter of port. After he had poured out a glass for himself and for me, he stood up.

'I feel I cannot allow this occasion to pass without proposing a toast,' he said, in his best public-dinner manner. 'I ask you to drink to the Commonwealth of Australia, and to our Benefactress who lives there, and who must assuredly be one of the kindest people in the world.'

'The Commonwealth of Australia, and our Benefactress!' I said, and we drained our glasses to the dregs.

Always your affectionate Childhood's Friend,

HENRIETTA

November 19, 1941

MY DEAR ROBERT
I am in London! Every year when autumn comes, and the bathing-dresses have been washed and put away, and the roof umbrella stowed in the cellar, and the cushions in the linen cupboard, I begin to long for London. I didn't go up at all last year, and this year the craving became so intense that at last I rushed to the telephone and

rang up Linda Dixon and asked her if she could have me to stay for two days, and that I'd bring a rabbit. Linda, who is the most welcoming person in the world, said it was just what she was longing for, and the rabbit wasn't necessary.

I was so pleased and excited I could only stammer and stutter down the telephone, but as soon as I had put the receiver back I began to have doubts. Suppose a bomb were to drop on Charles in my absence? Suppose a bomb were to drop on me in London? Charles and I hold strong views about being blown up together if we have to be blown up at all, and I had a vivid mental picture of Charles and the children in deep mourning, and Charles saying: 'She would go. I couldn't stop her. Your poor mother always had a craving for pleasure and excitement,' and an even worse one of me returning to find our house a smoking ruin surrounded by Charles's weeping patients.

'What's the matter?' said Charles after dinner. 'You seem very gloomy.'

'I'm going to London to-morrow.'

'I thought you wanted to go to London,' said Charles. 'You've been saying nothing else for a fortnight.'

'Well, now I'm going I sort of don't want to.'

Charles gave me a patient look. 'You always go on like this,' he said.

'Who's going to take Perry for his walkies?'

'Not me,' said Charles firmly, and opened *The Times*.

I woke up next morning with a heart like lead. Why, oh, why, had I deliberately let myself in for this agony? There was the telephone beside my bed. I lay and looked at it for a bit, and then picked up the receiver and asked for 'Trunks'.

'Linda, I'm not coming.'

'But why, darling?'

'Well, I just feel I can't.'

'Now, Henrietta,' said Linda firmly, 'I know exactly

how you feel, but you must fight against it. We shall expect you for tea.' Then she rang off.

As soon as I got out my suitcase Perry went and sat in it, looking at me very piteously. Charles said, 'Good-bye, old girl. Don't get run over in the black-out, you're such a fool in traffic.' Matins flung her arms round my neck and said, 'Oh, Madam, Madam, take care of yourself!' The man in the bank said, 'London? I hope we shall see you safely back, Mrs Brown.' Faith said, 'You'll have an awful journey,' and the Conductor said, 'London will make you cry.'

When I got to the station it was a shock to find that the twelve o'clock train now starts at twelve-thirty. Things are not what they were in the Old Country, Robert. But it gave me time to go back and fetch my earrings, which I had left on the mantelpiece. Matins, who thought I was my own ghost, uttered a loud shriek when she saw me, and dropped the dustpan and brush; and Perry, poor darling little Perry, who, like Mr Priestley, has his own ideas about Time, thought two days had passed, and gave me an ecstatic welcome.

It was almost worse getting off the second time, but I dragged myself away, and met Mrs Savernack in the road outside. 'You look very togged-up, Henrietta,' she said disapprovingly.

'I'm going to London, Mrs Savernack.'

'But we are asked not to travel.'

'I am going on business,' I said primly, looking down my nose, and left her staring.

This triumph over Mrs Savernack, my only one so far, did a lot to cheer me, and as I nearly missed my train and had to run from the top of the hill, there was no time for any more heart-burnings. Of course, directly I got in the train I began to enjoy myself, and, contrary to Faith's gloomy forebodings, I got a corner seat.

I nearly missed the train

As we slid into the suburbs, excitement clutched at my heart in the old way, but I found myself wondering whether I would get the same welcome as I used to. In the old days, London used to say, 'Here are the Autumn Visitors, give them a welcome,' and as you stepped out of the train, Waterloo Station bowed and smiled; but that was before the war. What was London going to say this time? Would she say, 'You are not a Londoner. Go back to the country where you belong, and don't come here to stare at my wounds'? I turned my eyes away from the devastation outside Waterloo, and fixed them on my book.

But London is just the same, Robert. As I drove away in my taxi, the autumn sunshine was on Westminster Bridge, and the tops of the houses loomed out of a faint grey mist, and there were dahlias in the park. Just the same, and unbelievably lovely. There are Gaps, of course, but even we in the West have Gaps, and after the first gasp of surprise and horror, one gets used to them. 'Here I am,' says London, 'knocked about a bit, but still here, and ready to give a welcome to a Country Cousin.'

When I was at Waterloo yesterday, Robert, I looked for you under the clock, and almost thought I could see you standing there. Where, like the Pale Hands somebody loved, are you now?

Always your affectionate Childhood's Friend,

HENRIETTA

December 3, 1941

M Y DEAR ROBERT
    Here I am, home again. Three days in London is not enough, but I must tell you of the exciting morning I had with Linda before I left.

Linda is a Salvage Adviser to a borough. When I said, 'How grand that sounds!' she turned those marvellous eyes on me and said simply, 'It *is* grand.' I really believe she is prouder of being a Salvage Adviser than she was of being the best Juliet ever seen on the English stage. Her job, as far as I can make out, is to go round to all the houses in the borough crying, 'Bring out your dead!' and then people rush out into the street with their old family teapots, or tear up the railings in the front garden, and Linda takes them away in a wheelbarrow. At least, that is what she told me, but one mustn't expect the unvarnished truth from people with imaginations.

Well, of course the Press soon got wind of these activities and came tearing round to the Salvage Head-quarters, baying like hounds. Linda told me she really *did* want to be an anonymous salvager, but as the matter was taken out of her hands she determined to give the *Evening Banner*, which was the paper which got the first refusal, so to speak, a run for its money.

That evening we went round to see Linda's two old great-aunts, Julia and Lucy, who live in a museum-piece house in a romantic square which is on Linda's salvage beat. Linda's aunts are the sort of regal and delightful old ladies of whom people say, 'They were intimate friends of Edward the Seventh, and he always went to tea there on Sunday afternoons.' They have a parlour-maid called Emerson who has been with them for fifty years—and now you know exactly the sort of house it is.

Linda was greeted rapturously at the front door by Emerson, and asked to see her aunts. We were shown into a room which had three original Landseers on the walls, and a mantelpiece draped with velvet. When Linda explained what she had come for, Aunts Julia and Lucy were on to it like lightning. It was easy to see from which side of the family Linda has inherited her dramatic talents.

'Will Emerson be all right?' said Linda.

'We will coach her in her part,' said Aunt Lucy.

The next morning we arrived in good time at the Salvage Headquarters. Linda was wearing a new hat, and the young men from the *Evening Banner* were practically speechless with excitement.

'This is my assistant, Mrs Brown,' said Linda, pointing at me. 'She accompanies me everywhere, for there are some streets in my district where No Woman Would Care To Go Alone.'

The Salvage City Father, who adores Linda and would never ask her to visit a Street Where No Woman Cares To Go Alone, besides having spent the best years of his life eliminating such streets from the borough, looked a little bleak at this, but sportingly said nothing.

The other young man took photographs of Linda—
(*a*) arriving at the office;
(*b*) sitting at her desk; and

(c) talking to the City Father.
After that we set out in a taxi.

'I always choose my house
by the window-curtains,' said
Linda as we drove into the
aunts' square.

'There's a good one,'
said the reporter pointing.

'No, I think this one,'
said Linda firmly, and the taxi
drew up at her aunts' door.

Emerson answered the
door, wearing spectacles and
with her cap a little crooked.
'I am the Salvage Adviser,'
said Linda. 'Is your mistress
at home?'

Arriving at the office

'I doubt whether they'll see you,' said Emerson, in a
strange, unnatural voice.

'Oh, please,' said Linda, with the smile that used to
bring the gallery cheering to its feet. It was on this occasion
noted, in shorthand, by the reporter in his little book.

We were shown into the drawing-room. Emerson
retreated hastily, and there was a noise like a sneeze as she
shut the door. Aunt Julia was sitting in a high-backed chair,
doing tatting, and Aunt Lucy was playing 'The Last Rose
of Summer' on the piano, which was very out of tune.

'I am the Salvage Adviser,' said Linda, in a rather
shaky voice. 'Is there any salvage you can let me have to
help Old England in her hour of need?'

Aunts Julia and Lucy rose to their feet and stood
side by side in dignified silence. Then Aunt Julia spoke.
'My dear,' she said, 'my sister and I are in very reduced
circumstances.'

'Nearly all our possessions,' said Aunt Lucy sadly,

looking round the overcrowded room, 'have come under the auctioneer's hammer to pay our debts.'

'But England's call has never gone unheeded in this house,' said Aunt Julia, and she went to a corner-cabinet and took out a pair of handsome Sheffield-plate candlesticks which she handed to Linda. 'They were given to our father by Disraeli,' she said simply.

Then Aunt Lucy went to the writing-desk and unlocked a drawer. She took out a little bundle of letters tied with pink ribbon. 'Please take them,' she said, and pressed them into Linda's hands.

The other young man took a lot of photographs, and we were asked to partake of gooseberry wine. This was served by Emerson in long-stemmed glasses and the other young man took yet another photograph. I don't know what the gooseberry wine was, but there was a lot of gin in it, and we parted hilariously on the steps of the Salvage Office.

'You're a grand showman, Miss Linda Larcombe,' said the reporter, and I rather think there was a twinkle in his eye.

We took the candlesticks and the little bundle of letters back after tea. 'Darlings, you were *magnificent*,' said Linda, kissing them warmly, 'and what *did* you do to the piano?'

'I unscrewed some of those knobs inside with the pliers,' said Aunt Julia.

'And are those really love-letters, Aunt Lucy?'

Aunt Lucy smiled. 'There are six volumes of your grandfather's sermons waiting for your salvage if you like to call for them in the morning,' she said.

Always your affectionate Childhood's Friend,

HENRIETTA

December 31, 1941

M Y DEAR ROBERT
Neither Bill nor the Linnet got home for Christmas this year, and Lady B, who always dines with us on Christmas Day, was in bed with a cold, poor darling, so Charles and I decided to give Evensong the night off, and have a quiet cottage pie. On Christmas morning I gave Charles a pair of sock-suspenders, and he gave me a pair of nail-scissors. We thanked each other gravely, and went to our respective tasks as usual. Matins had given herself the morning off, and people are always iller than usual on Christmas Day. Charles rushed in for lunch, and rushed out again twenty minutes later with a set expression on his face.

In the afternoon I went to see Lady B, who wouldn't let me into her room because of germs. So I went back home, lit the fire in the drawing-room, did the black-out all over the house and sat down with my knitting. At six o'clock there was a lot of scuffling and scrunching on the path outside, and some children began singing carols. We get a lot of carols here, most of them squeaked hurriedly through the letter-box, but these were real carols, sung by a lot of children with a grown-up in charge.

'God Rest You Merrie, Gentlemen', they sang in their clear, sweet voices, and very nearly in tune. After that, we had 'Once in Royal David's City', and 'No-well, No-well'. A very small child came in with the collecting-box, and deeply moved by their performance, I gave, as they say, generously. When Charles came home he found me sitting in the dark, blowing my nose.

'You're not getting a cold, are you?' he said, rather crossly, as he switched on the lights. 'Hullo!' he said, peering at me closely, 'what's going on here?'

'It was the carols,' I muttered.

'But carols oughtn't to make you sad.'

'Well, these did. There is so little, so very little peace and good will in the world just now, Charles.'

165

Charles patted me kindly on the shoulder. 'Not the international sort, perhaps. Plenty of individual good will,' he said. 'And now go and put that cottage pie in the oven, I'm hungry.'

When I got back, I found Charles surrounded by a great many strange bottles. He handed me a glass of pale amber-coloured liquid. 'Drink that,' he said. 'It'll get you where you live.'

I took a sip. 'Charles!' I said. 'What ever is it made of?'

'Remnants,' said Charles, with an airy wave of the hand towards the imposing array of bottles on the piano. 'How does it taste?'

'Potent, but nice.'

'Good. Have another.'

'Thank you, Charles.'

'You know, Henrietta,' said Charles, as he refilled his glass and mine, 'even if we can buy the ingredients, we shall never be able to have this drink again, because I can't remember how I made it. It is gone for ever, like the Lost Chord. "It may be that only in heav'n ... "'

'Damn Hitler!' I said loudly.

'Hear, hear!' said Charles. 'And the Japs.'

'And Musso, and Laval.'

'And God bless the King.'

'The King!'

'And the Queen.'

'Wait a minute, old girl, while I fill up my glass. Now then. And the Queen, God bless her! And the little Princesses.'

'Absent friends, Charles.'

'Absent friends, coupled with the names of Bill and Linnet Brown,' said Charles.

'And the Americans.'

'Your glass is empty, Henrietta. May I give you a little more?'

'Thank you, Charles. Just a drop. I find your mixture delicious, but a trifle strong.'

'There you are. Now, where were we?'

'The Americans.'

'Good luck to them.'

'And the Choles and Pecks.'

Charles gave me a keen look. 'The Poles and Czechs, and all our other allies,' he said firmly, and brought our toasting to a timely end.

'I feel better,' I said.

'That was the idea,'said Charles modestly.

'A Merry Christmas, Charles.'

'The same to you, Henrietta.'

We went in to dinner arm-in-arm, and Charles said it was the most delicious cottage pie he had ever had.

Always your affectionate Childhood's Friend,

HENRIETTA

'And the Choles and Pecks'